'You deserve to be whipped for that,' Melik snarled savagely.

'Oh, so now we're back to the old days all of a sudden, are we?' Louisa asked bitingly. 'As soon as you meet with a little resistance, a woman who doesn't see things your way, it's back to the sultan approach with force and whips? Charming, absolutely charming.'

Dear Reader

We have a real treat for you this month! Helen Brooks takes you on a magic carpet to the fascinating country of Turkey. Like her, you'll find that it's always full of surprises, from its mountains and lush forest to its lively, bustling cities, quiet, unspoilt beaches and ruins haunted by the ghosts of many turbulent centuries. Whether you're interested in the fascinating past or the exciting present, we're sure that your stay will be a romantic one. . .!

The Editor

The author says:

'Glittering sunlight flashing off the golden crescents of domed mosques, exotic sultans' palaces and colourful Eastern bazaars, beautiful sandy beaches lapped by clear seas of a brilliant blue. . . If, like me, this is the picture the word "Turkey" conjures up for you, rest assured it is that and much, much more. It's a land of enormous contrasts, inhabited by people whose generosity and kindness is only matched by their warm hospitality. Visit Turkey. . .and enter a dream!'

Helen Brooks

★ TURN TO THE BACK PAGES OF THIS BOOK FOR *WELCOME TO EUROPE*. . .OUR FASCINATING FACT-FILE ★

THE SULTAN'S FAVOURITE

BY

HELEN BROOKS

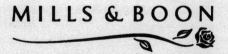

MILLS & BOON LIMITED
ETON HOUSE, 18–24 PARADISE ROAD
RICHMOND, SURREY, TW9 1SR

*MILLS & BOON and the Rose Device
are trademarks of the publisher.*

*First published in Great Britain 1994
by Mills & Boon Limited*

© Helen Brooks 1994

*Australian copyright 1994   Philippine copyright 1994
This edition 1994*

ISBN 0 263 78575 0

Set in 10 on 12 pt Linotron Times
01-9408-53679

*Typeset in Great Britain by Centracet, Cambridge
Made and printed in Great Britain*

CHAPTER ONE

'CAN I be of assistance?' As the deep, lazy voice with its faint accent sounded just behind her, Louisa swung round in surprise, her arms full of the rich, vibrant silk and her dark velvety brown eyes wide with a mixture of apprehension and annoyance. Not another intended pick-up? In the two weeks since she had been in Istanbul the sheer persistence of a certain section of the male population had astounded her.

'I beg your pardon?' Her voice was deliberately cool and remote but even as she spoke she realised her mistake, her cheeks flushing a faint pink. This man was not out of the same mould as the fancy-free youths who assumed a young female on her own was looking for a little diversion which they were only too happy to supply. He was tall, very tall, dark and exquisitely dressed in a pale grey suit and silk shirt that shouted intimidating wealth, and as his eyes locked on to hers the jolt she received was stunning.

'You seem to be having a little difficulty?' She heard him speak but for the life of her was unable to respond. He was devastatingly handsome and wickedly male, the wide, strong shoulders set at an angle that pro-claimed overpowering confidence in his virility and ability to command, but it was his eyes that dried up the words in her throat and were rendering her help-less. He was so dark she would have expected his eyes to be black, maybe grey but almost certainly brown to fit in with the shining ebony hair, but the vivid tawny-gold eyes flecked with an iridescent green were as mesmerising as those of a big cat and just as deadly.

The slightly ironic twist to the hard mouth suddenly informed her she was staring with her mouth half-open and still without having made any coherent reply. 'It's all right, thank you,' she said quickly, lowering her eyes in confusion as she half turned back to the small beady-eyed shopkeeper she had been bargaining with for the beautiful peach-coloured silk shawl. 'I don't need any help.'

'You do not?' The rich voice was openly disbelieving and as he shot some rapid Turkish at the attentive little trader watching them both so closely she saw the man's sharp-featured face melt into an ingratiating smile.

'*Evet effendi, evet.*' He nodded vigorously. '*Mersi, mersi.*'

'The item is yours.'

'What?' In a daze she watched an inordinate amount of lira change hands before she could move, and then as realisation washed over her in a burning wave she raised her head sharply, her soft brown eyes flashing fire. 'Now just hang on a moment! I don't know if I can afford this and——'

'The shawl is a gift, a humble token of my admiration for your beauty.' It was an outrageous line but somehow in the exotic confines of Istanbul's famous Covered Bazaar it fitted perfectly. 'The only thing I would ask in return is to be allowed to know your name.' His voice was low and husky and touched with the faintest lilt of an accent, and Louisa felt the shiver that started somewhere in the region of her spine travel all the way to her toes. How old was he? she thought irrelevantly as she stared back into narrowed eyes watching her so intently. A touch of white at his temples and the laughter-lines cut deep into the tanned, clear skin put his age in the late thirties, maybe even forty; the taut, powerful body was giving nothing away.

'Look, this is ridiculous, Mr. . .?' With a tremendous effort she pulled herself together. 'I can't possibly accept a present from a perfect stranger and I doubt if I can afford the shawl myself. Could you just ask for your money back or something. . .?'

Her voice died away as he threw back his head in laughter. 'My name is Melik, my hot-tempered enchantress with eyes of midnight, and no, I cannot "just ask for my money back". That would be extremely rude and quite out of the question. You have to decide whether to make this shop owner the unworthy recipient of an undeserved bonus or to allow me the pleasure of a purely spontaneous action with no thought of compromise or ungentlemanly motives on my side, I assure you. You are very beautiful; I know of no one at the moment more suited to be clothed in the richness of silk, so. . .?' He smiled slowly with a trace of dark amusement lighting the feline eyes as they wandered over her hot face. 'I would be most honoured if you would accept the gift.'

'I don't believe this.' She gazed helplessly down the street packed full of shops and tiny cubby-holes rich with silk, lace, cotton and a thousand other materials made into beautiful shawls, gossamer-thin dresses, pretty blouses and every other item of clothing possible to imagine, with the traders sitting in front of their wares like patient spiders waiting to pounce.

The Bazaar was a small city in itself, over four thousand shops of varying sizes from tiny one-stalled indentations to large, impressive glass-plated establishments in the more opulent sections where the jeweller's shops stood shoulder to shoulder displaying their glittering bounty. Each section was devoted to its own trade and she had wandered through the vast maze, all under one roof, without any clear intention to buy until she had spotted the delicate, exotically patterned shawl in rich fine silk in one small shop. She wished with all her heart now that she had stayed at the apartment.

'Is it too dreadful a thing to contemplate?' She felt the laughter in the dark voice even though his face was politely grave now. 'Can you not look on it as a delightful diversion out of the normal rush of life?'

'But——' She stopped abruptly as her eyes were drawn back to his. What should she do? He had bought the shawl now, the trader had pocketed the money immediately, his eyes flashing from one to the other as his teeth exposed themselves in a knowing smile; it was a *fait accompli* and yet she couldn't, she just couldn't accept it. . .

'Come.' The decision was suddenly taken out of her hands as the tall stranger took the bag the trader was proffering in one hand, her arm in the other, and walked a few paces down the street before she pulled herself free.

'I'm not going anywhere with you.' There was real fear in her face now even as she forced her voice to remain steady. 'Just take your shawl and go away. I'll call for help——'

'I do not think the shawl is quite my colour.' He couldn't hide the laughter that was shaking his voice and as she glared up at him he made a visible effort to control his amusement. 'I apologise, little tigress—I can imagine how this must seem. If it helps at all you have my word that I am as surprised by my actions as you undoubtedly are. I do not make it a habit to buy strange women gifts of any sort but I had been watching you for some time and I wanted to make contact.' The direct honesty took her breath away, coupled as it was with the totally disarming smile that softened the cruel eyes and hard mouth. 'I would like to buy you a coffee, maybe talk a little, but the decision is yours. Say the word and I will disappear like the frost before the first breath of summer.'

'Well. . .' She glanced again at the exquisite hand-made suit and soft leather shoes. He was obviously a wealthy businessman idling away a couple of hours between engagements, and the situation had got ridic-ulous. A coffee wouldn't hurt and then she could say goodbye quickly and cleanly but the shawl was staying with him come hell or high water! She didn't doubt for a minute that there were plenty of female 'friends' he could give it to! 'A quick coffee, then, but I really can't accept the shawl although it was very kind of you.' She smiled carefully and coolly, her eyes guarded.

'Kind?' The sweep of his lashes made her stomach muscles tighten with a strange foreboding. 'I am not a kind man, Miss. . .?'

'Collins. Louisa Collins,' she said quickly.

'Louisa. . .' He let her name trail over his lips sensuously. 'I like this name; it suits you.'

'Thank you.' She stared at him helplessly, feeling like a schoolgirl totally out of her depth instead of a grown woman of twenty-eight perfectly in control of her own life. 'This is crazy. . .' She shook her blonde head as they began to walk.

She didn't realise she had spoken out loud until he smiled mockingly. 'Isn't it,' he agreed lightly. 'But surely one is allowed a little madness occasionally?'

As she met his eyes again, her mouth rueful, she

caught a flash of something hot and bright deep in their gold depths that suddenly caused the blood to pound through her veins madly. It had been hungry, voracious, something quite out of keeping with the persuasive talk and smiling banter, as though a carefully constructed mask had slipped for a brief moment to reveal a fierce volcanic primitive force that was supremely powerful and intrinsically cruel. What was she doing? She almost stopped as her mind raced. She shouldn't even be having coffee with this man. He was dangerous — her sixth sense had picked up something that the layers of civilisation couldn't quite hide — and he wanted her. She knew it as clearly as though he had voiced it and it wasn't false vanity. Her sixth sense also told her he wasn't a man who liked to be thwarted.

'No second thoughts, Miss Collins.' The razor-sharp mind had picked up her agitation somehow. 'I have always understood that an Englishman's word is his bond and I am sure that applies to the female of the species. Now, let us take a nice stroll to a little coffee-shop I know that is quite delightful. Have you been to Ic Bedesten?'

'Ic Bedesten?' She shook her head. 'I'm sorry, I don't understand——'

'The old bazaar.' His face was reassuringly bland now and she took herself to task firmly. He had only asked her to have coffee, for goodness' sake! He was obviously disgustingly wealthy with film-star good looks to boot; he'd have the women fighting a path to his door, and here was she thinking he was interested in her! She almost smiled. Stop imagining things, Louisa, and enjoy the moment, she told herself crossly; there haven't been too many to enjoy for some time after all. The ever-present cloud that had lifted during the last few minutes settled again as she remembered, and as the man at her side glanced at her closed face his own darkened quizzically.

'Louisa? There is something wrong?'

'Wrong?' She smiled quickly. 'Of course not, and no, I haven't been to the old bazaar, or I don't think I have! Is it different from this?'

'The old bazaar is at the centre of this maze,' he said quietly as his eyes searched her face. 'The jumble of centuries is located there — rusty swords and old camel bells, ancient tiles painted with texts in Arabic calligraphy and a million and one other secrets that have been unearthed through time and man's greed. Occasionally a treasure is found and a fortune made; I will take you there one day,' he finished in the same breath. 'It is the real bazaar, a taste of the past.'

One day? She forced her expression to reveal nothing even as mind and body protested. One day? Over her dead body! This was definitely a one-off. She didn't need any complications in her life; she was too bruised and raw for that, and this man was far too. . . uncomfortable. A coffee, a brief chat and then a parting of the ways.

Although protected from the fierce rays of the September sun by its roof, the sixty-seven streets of the bazaar were warm and humid in the Turkish heat, the highly coloured sights, exotic spiced smells and crowded streets and alleys alive with the taste of the orient, Istanbullus shopping for daily essentials alongside rich American tourists. As they reached the tiny coffee-shop set slightly back from the street Louisa found her feet were aching and she sank gratefully on to the small upholstered seat Melik indicated, smoothing back a wisp of bright golden hair that had escaped from the tight knot at the back of her head as she did so.

'Why do you try and hide such beauty?' he asked her softly as his eyes followed the gesture. 'Your hair should be your glory, is this not so?'

'I prefer to keep it under control,' she said shortly. 'It's too curly and there's too much of it.'

'You are a strange young woman, Louisa Collins,' he said after a long moment. 'If it weren't so ridiculous in one so lovely I would almost think you are frightened of life.'

'Frightened?' She eyed him angrily now, her thin brown brows drawing together in a frown. 'You're right, it is ridiculous.' She raised her chin defiantly.

'Maybe.' He smiled easily although this time it didn't touch the hard gold of his eyes. 'And maybe not. Nevertheless you do not have the look of a woman who has been kissed recently; am I right?' He stood looking down at her from his great height, his arms folded, legs slightly apart, his whole manner one of male domination, and she felt hot rage flood her chest. How dared he? How dared he question her like this? A virtual stranger probing into her life!

'I don't really think that's any of your business,' she said coldly, her cheeks scarlet. 'Do you?'

'On the contrary.' He was blatantly unaffected by her rage; she was furious to notice that there was even a slight twist to his mouth as he surveyed her angry face as though he was finding it all most amusing. 'It is quite immoral to think that a woman as beautiful as you is not enjoying the pleasures of love at night in the arms of her lover. I dislike waste in any form.'

'Oh, you——' She was still spluttering for words as he leant forward and touched her hot cheek gently with the tip of one finger, his eyes lingering for a moment on her parted lips before he brushed them lightly with his own. She leapt back in her seat as though she had been scalded, shocked to find that that light pressure had ignited a host of feelings totally alien to her that ran from the top of her head to the soles of her feet.

'Coffee.' He drew back smoothly, his tawny gaze like fire on her skin. 'I have to make a telephone call; I am already late for an appointment. I will not be long.' He indicated a partly concealed telephone booth at the back of the shop with a nonchalant wave of his hand. 'I will arrange for coffee and pastries to be sent over so you will not be disturbed, and then on my return we will continue this interesting conversation, yes?'

'I wasn't aware that we were having a conversation,' she said stiffly as she forced herself to sit perfectly still and hide the trembling that was threatening to become visible at any moment. 'And I've no intention of tolerating any more questions of a personal nature, Mr Melik.'

'Melik is my first name,' he said softly, his narrowed eyes flicking over her stony face with a piercing light that seemed to reach out to her very soul, 'and why so threatened, Louisa? I'm not going to hurt you.' His gaze lingered on the pale cream of her skin before moving to the pure gold hair so tightly confined in its pins. 'You are a very beautiful woman — many men must have told you this — added to which you have an elegance, a confidence that only comes with maturity and is far more sensual than any girlish shyness. Can we not talk as equals?'

She dragged her eyes away from his dark face, quite unable to reply. He had assumed she was a woman of the world, cool, poised and able to take care of herself in any romantic situation, and she had to admit that was exactly the effect she liked to give. It was her protection, her safeguard in the male-dominated world she had chosen to work in, but it went far deeper than that. But she would not, she *could not* explain herself to him! Let him think what he liked; she wouldn't ever see him again after today anyway, and maybe it was better if he saw her as a composed career woman with a cool head on her shoulders and a mind to match.

'As equals?' It took every ounce of her will to smile quietly into the eagle-eyed handsome face watching her so closely. 'I wouldn't have thought a Turkish man would encourage such presumption from a mere woman!'

'You have been reading too many novels, Louisa,' he said silkily, the inflexion he gave her name causing that now familiar shiver to travel down her spine. 'The days of the harems are long since gone but even in those times there was more power wielded in one pair of tiny hands weighed down with rings and bracelets than in the hand holding the sword. Make no mistake, just because my countrymen have always appreciated a woman's beauty, it does not mean that they have ignored her intelligence and wisdom.'

'Really?' She eyed him with scornful disbelief and his mouth tightened.

'Really,' he said coldly. 'Turkish men treat their womenfolk with great respect; in fact a woman travelling alone in my country is safer than in many other countries including your own.'

'So you're saying you're interested in a woman's mind first?' She realised her mistake immediately. The hard eyes softened into a smile and the sensual mouth twisted slightly as his gaze wandered over her flushed face.

'I would not like to be guilty of such deception,' he said gravely, 'especially where you are concerned. Nevertheless you are a person as a whole, mind, soul and body, as I am. This I would respect.'

As a smiling waiter appeared at their elbows Melik spoke swiftly in fluent Turkish before turning to her again, his expression slightly preoccupied. 'I really must make that telephone call, if you will excuse me? This is the first time I have played the—how you say? Hookey?—in a long, long time.' He smiled warmly. 'But I could not resist such temptation. My mind, soul *and* body responded to the call.'

She leant back in the small seat as she looked up at him, her eyes steady even as her heartbeat raced. He was so good-looking, so sure of himself even when he was mocking her like now. What would it be like to be loved by a man like this? The thought shocked her; she could only view it as a betrayal of Oliver, and she lowered her eyes quickly as a small pulse beat agitatedly in her throat. 'That's fine. Please, make the call.'

As he walked away, his big, lean body towering over the other occupants of the small, deliciously scented coffee-shop, she felt herself begin to shake as the urge to escape became paramount. He was too much, she thought desperately. Too big, too aggressively masculine, too savage, the very antithesis of Oliver, in fact. He belonged to a different age, a golden age of all-powerful sultans majestic and terrible in their cruelty and infinitely skilful in the arts of love. A warm ache followed the trembling into her lower stomach. She didn't like him, she didn't like him at all, and she liked still less the flickers of fear that were sending shivers all over her body. Or was it fear? That thought galvanised her feet into action as she cast a quick glance across the room.

She was just beginning to get herself together again and she couldn't risk having the peace of mind, fought for at such cost over the last few months, casually destroyed by this insufferable, dominantly male stranger with his probing questions and strange cat-like eyes. 'I won't allow it,' she muttered desperately to herself as her eyes fastened on his hard profile across the room. He was talking with intense concentration into the receiver and she seized the opportunity like a tiny caged bird who saw the door swinging open. She was out in the street almost without being aware of it and then she was running, blindly and with the breath rasping in her throat, until the mad headlong flight was stopped when she crashed into a huge pile of intricately weaved baskets outside one of the shops several streets away.

The shopkeeper was immediately to hand, waving aside her apologies with smiles and bows and offering her the inevitable cup of tea with which the traders tempted all prospective buyers into their shops.

'Please.' She almost clutched hold of the small man's tunic as she spoke. 'I need to get out of here quickly; which way do I go?' If she saw him again now she would die of embarrassment; whatever had possessed her to leave like that?

'*Efendim*.' The little man bowed as he spoke, his eyes concerned as they took in her white face. 'You are in trouble, you need help?'

'I just need to get out of here.' She gestured wildly. 'Which way is quickest?'

It seemed hours before she stepped out of the bazaar

into the hot September air but in reality was only several minutes, but it wasn't until she was safe in a taxi speeding crazily along the busy streets of the huge city that she dared to relax, the breath leaving her body in a long deep sigh as she leant back against the plastic-covered seat.

She was mad! She should have stayed! What if she ran into him again? What would she say? Her thoughts continued to tumble crazily over one another until at last, as always, the magic of Istanbul, that most romantic of cities, soothed her. Three thousand years ago a small fishing village on the headland between the mouth of the Golden Horn and the Sea of Marmara, kept cool in the blinding heat of summer by welcome sea breezes, and now a beautiful city bursting at the seams with exotic domed mosques, sultans' palaces and Eastern bazaars, its appeal was timeless. The whole bustling labyrinth was a fascinating mixture of East and West, old and new, a rich and colourful legacy from its past position as the capital of three world empires.

'You like Istanbul, eh? Is good, maybe?' The taxi driver turned round with a toothless beam, having noticed her rapt contemplation of the whirling scene outside his window, and like all the taxi drivers she had met so far seemed quite oblivious to the fast and furious traffic surging along all around them.

'Very good,' she agreed quickly, sagging with relief as he turned back to the wheel.

When she had first arrived two weeks ago, heartsore and more than a little apprehensive, the busy port city had overwelmed her with its contrasts, Byzantine brilliance and Ottoman opulence blending with poor shabby houses and back-street alleys, the sirens of ships often competing with the ancient timeless sound of muezzins calling the faithful to prayer. But she loved it now. She hugged her knees as she gazed out of the gleaming window. It had reached something deep inside her, touching a passion for the past that she had never known existed. And the Turkish people must be the most friendly and genuine race on the planet, she reflected soberly; it was true what Melik had said. . . The thought of him brought her bolt upright again. Well, that little interlude was over now and best forgotten! She hadn't handled it very well, on reflection, but it had been his fault! She hadn't wanted a tête-à-tête with anyone, least of all a dashing golden-eyed Turk who had had more than his fair share of cheek!

She relaxed again slowly as the taxi neared the end of its race to her apartment block. That was it; it had been nothing more than a brief amusing interval in her undeniably busy life. Amusing? Somehow the word didn't quite fit the emotions that were still keeping the blood hot in her cheeks and the butterflies dancing crazily everywhere else. And she'd keep it to herself! She nodded slowly, unaware of the taxi driver's appreciative glance on her soft, creamy skin, flushed cheeks and bright eyes. She somehow couldn't share this episode with anyone and she would never see him again anyway. It was best forgotten and locked away and she wouldn't, she *wouldn't* think about him any more.

CHAPTER TWO

'OH, wow! *Who* is that? He's absolutely gorgeous!' As Louisa followed Sandra's eyes across the crowded office her own widened with horror. It couldn't be! She must be mistaken. She shut her eyes tightly for a moment as she took a long deep breath to calm her racing heart. It wasn't Melik, just someone who looked like him, and she had interposed the devastating features she had dreamt about every night for a week on this other man's face.

She opened her eyes again cautiously but the man standing in the doorway talking to her boss had moved slightly and his face was turned from her. All that was visible was a slight glimpse of one tanned cheek, jet-black straight hair gleaming with health in the harsh artificial light overhead, and the tall, broad-shouldered body that dwarfed little Mr Ashton into a tiny gnome.

'Dephni?' Sandra leant over backwards from the large desk she shared with Louisa and whispered an aside to the little Turkish girl next to her without taking her eyes off the remote figure in the doorway. 'That man, the one with Mr Ashton, who is he?'

As Dephni's large liquid eyes glanced across the room they dropped immediately back to the work at her fingertips as she shook her head slightly. 'I speak with you later, Sandra.'

Sandra made a face at Louisa as she turned back into her seat, adequately expressing her opinion of the other girl's reticence. 'Well, he's a dreamboat anyway,' she muttered longingly as, leaning on her elbows, she let her eyes take their fill. 'A real-life, Technicolor dreamboat. . .'

'Sandra, you'll be in hot water again.' Louisa's voice was low and full of meaning as she caught her friend's eye and indicated Mrs Jones, Mr Ashton's dragon of a secretary, who was following the two men into Mr Ashton's private office after a cursory glance at the rest of the office. Damn! She'd missed the opportunity to have a good look at his face, listening to Sandra's ramblings, but it couldn't be him, not here, not in the office.

'How can you think of work with such a vision only yards away?' Sandra whispered dramatically, rolling her big blue eyes heavenwards. 'I mean he's gorgeous, *really* gorgeous!'

'Because that's what we were brought over from England to do,' Louisa returned drily, blessing the fact that her inner agitation wasn't showing on her face. She looked down at her hands resting on the desk and was annoyed to see that they were trembling slightly. This was ridiculous! It wasn't even him and she didn't *want* it to be either, did she? No, she didn't! Of course she didn't.

'Twelve months in Turkey and getting paid for it.' Sandra was still muttering away at her elbow. 'There's always a catch, though, even in paradise, and Mrs Jones is certainly it in this case. She's determined herself as a cross between a guardian angel and a chaperon and she's spoiling all our fun. I haven't even had a goodnight kiss in the three weeks we've been here; she's driving me mad. It's all work, work, work. The woman's obsessed with it.'

'Sandra. . .' Louisa's voice was flat. Her thoughts

were racing and she really couldn't take Sandra grumbling in her ear at this precise moment in time.

'Oh, it's all right for you!' Sandra flicked her head sulkily. 'Mrs Jones knows you don't want to meet anyone, so she doesn't bother with you. She knows you'll be content to die an old maid——' She stopped abruptly, her eyes stricken. 'Oh, I'm sorry, Lou, I didn't mean that really. I'm such a pig.'

'Yes, you are.' Louisa smiled brightly to hide the hurt the other girl's words had caused. 'But I'll put it down to frustration this time.' As Sandra smiled gratefully and lowered her head to her work, Louisa tried to concentrate on her bulging file of data, but it was impossible—her mind was flitting all over the place.

Thursday, September the tenth. The tiny date window on Oliver's gold watch, slightly incongruous on her small, delicate wrist but which she wore with fierce pride, reminded her yet again of the fact she had been struggling with all week along with the acutely disturbing dreams that seemed to mock her daytime reflections. This would have been her honeymoon. . . As hot tears pricked the back of her eyes she cautioned herself sternly. Don't think of it, not now, not here. Later.

'Miss Collins?' She hadn't been aware of Mrs Jones crossing the office but now the other woman's voice brought her head snapping upwards. It was the general opinion among the staff of Lectron Technics that the managing director's secretary was the real power behind the throne and it was well known that she had personally hand-picked the chosen few for the Turkish project. Although formidable, the middle-aged lady was both perceptive and extremely intelligent, and now, as the iron-grey eyes met Louisa's nervous gaze, they were not unfriendly. 'Could you spare a moment, please? In Mr Ashton's office?'

For a crazy moment Louisa thought about refusing but then common sense prevailed over blind panic. It wasn't him! Of course it wasn't him and she couldn't decline the order disguised as a request anyway.

The slashed rays of sunlight filtering through the blinds at the windows turned Louisa's head into blazing gold as she followed Mrs Jones across the room, her pencil-slim skirt and neat white blouse unable to hide the tiny waist, full breasts and long legs that had more than one pair of male eyes following their progress in predatory interest.

'If I could just explain, my dear?' Once inside the small ante-room where Mrs Jones had her desk the older woman put a restraining hand on Louisa's arm, turning her round to face the wall so that they both had their backs to the general workforce. 'The gentleman with Mr Ashton that Sandra noticed?' Louisa grimaced inwardly; those sharp grey eyes didn't miss a thing! 'It's Mr Haman—*the* Mr Haman,' she added with slight emphasis.

Louisa tried to look suitably impressed, which wasn't difficult as her stomach churned at the mention of the great man's name. This, then, was the Turkish-French millionaire that Lectron were entering into partnership with? The demanding, obstreperous individual who had the future of countless jobs hanging on his precarious whims and fancies? This was one man she would prefer not to meet. She had heard——

'Now I don't know what you've heard, Miss Collins,' Mrs Jones continued quietly, 'but no doubt it's all been grossly exaggerated—you know what the office grapevine is like at the best of times. Our agent, Mr Pasha, speaks very highly of him.'

Louisa nodded politely without replying. Mrs Jones knew as well as she did from the correspondence she had dealt with since the project was first envisaged that Mr Haman had been the very devil of a man to deal with. After the prices had been negotiated by careful tender over long, tedious months and finally agreed, he had been adamant that he have the final say in sources and funding despite the English reservations that if the Turkish source should run into difficulties they would be left high and dry. Once committed the English funding was irrevocable and delays of a few days could cost the firm dearly.

Mr Haman had swept all objections aside, insisting that he had access to credit and grants that would suffice in all emergencies despite the red-tape bureaucracy that was forever rearing its head. Most of the items that Lectron would be dealing with were on the Turkish restricted list for which permission must be sought, and although the specialist agent, Zengi Pasha, had been invaluable, Lectron were still seeing bogeymen behind every door. It had all made for tense relations and to date Mr Haman had not proved a patient or sympathetic observer of any hesitation or nervousness on Lectron's part.

'When we enter I will introduce you and then you will sit quietly in the seat indicated while Mr Ashton explains what is required of you. There will be no need for you to make any comment or venture an opinion. Is that understood?'

Louisa stared in astonishment at the other woman's face, noticing for the first time the tell-tale stain of pink colouring the strong cheekbones and the faint tic beating under one eye. She was nervous! The thought was so mind-boggling that Louisa's mouth opened slightly in wonder. In the six years she had worked for Lectron since leaving college with a fairly mediocre degree she had never, ever seen Mrs Jones other than perfectly poised and in charge.

Had Mr Haman wrought the miracle? In that case she was even more sure she didn't want to meet him! If he could cause the esteemed Mrs Jones to develop an attack of the vapours, how was he going to affect *her*?

'Miss Collins? Do you understand? This is important.' There was a shrill note in the normally rather masculine voice that emphasised over-tight nerves.

'I'm sorry, Mrs Jones,' Louisa answered automatically, still staring at the secretary's long face. 'Yes, of course I understand. I won't say anything at all unless directly spoken to.' And I'll curtsy first, she thought wryly.

'Fine, fine, I knew you'd understand.' Mrs Jones looked anxiously at the closed door. 'You're a very reliable girl, Miss Collins, very reliable.' The severe mouth allowed itself a faint twist that was meant to serve as a smile. 'Come along.'

Louisa had only been admitted to the inner sanctum that the rest of the office irreverently called the 'holy of holies' once, and then Mrs Jones had whisked her in and out at the speed of light although she had gained an impression of beautifully worked Turkish carpets covering the polished wood floor, shiny antique furniture and an overall feeling of luxury quite at odds with the spartan comfort in the main office.

The building itself was magnificent, one of the old palaces dotted throughout Istanbul that had been crumbling gracefully away until restored by a hopeful entrepreneur into a somewhat regal office building of which Lectron occupied the second floor along with Mr Haman's employees.

'Ah, Mrs Jones and Miss. . .' Mr Ashton let his reedy voice fade away as Mrs Jones made the necessary introductions, but Louisa neither heard nor felt anything beyond a racing buzzing in her ears and a surge of blinding adrenalin had her heart leaping out of her chest as her gaze met the tawny-gold eyes that had haunted her for long restless nights.

Close to, Melik Haman seemed even larger than she remembered, the tanned, hard-planed face cruel and sardonic as he savoured her horror and confusion, his eyes narrowed slits of light that gleamed with deadly brightness.

This was it, then! It was the first coherent thought to surface out of the panic. She'd be straight back to England post-haste and very possibly straight out of a job there too! Strangely the realisation brought her head up and her shoulders back and as she stared back at him, her eyes turned into dark ebony full of defiance. Go on, then, they spoke into the cat-like gaze fixing her to the spot, have your revenge, get the fun over with. Her chin rose a fraction higher.

'Miss. . .Collins, I think the name was?' It was the same deep, rich, cool voice as before but with a hard edge to it that hadn't been there previously.

She nodded slowly, her eyes fixed on his like a rabbit before a snake.

'Yes. . .I like that name.' He turned to Mr Ashton with a cold smile. 'For some reason it appealed to me when you read me the list of possible assistants.'

'Good, good.' Mr Ashton was almost rubbing his

hands in gratification. 'Anything we can do, Melik, anything at all. You only have to ask. I can't apologise enough but you understand the circumstances?'

'Calm yourself, John.' The ruthless gaze switched back to Louisa and she just stopped herself flinching in time. 'Are you acquainted with the circumstances?'

'What?' She stared at him blankly as her mind went into hyper-drive. He wasn't going to denounce her, then? Insist on her immediate dismissal? For a moment heady relief swamped all other sensation and then an icy trickle shivered down her spine. Why not? He would be furious at the trick she had, almost unwittingly, played on him, and it wasn't in this man's nature to be forgiving. She knew that as surely as she drew breath.

'I thought it would be better for you to explain,' Mrs Jones interposed hastily with a swift glance at Mr Ashton. 'But I can——'

'Would you like me to explain the position we find ourselves in, Miss Collins?' He cut across Mrs Jones's voice as though she hadn't spoken and the older woman immediately fell silent. In other circumstances Louisa would have felt like giving such courage recognition but just at this moment in time she was struggling to remain upright.

'Take a seat, Miss Collins.' He had seen the trembling in her legs, she just knew it, and although she would have given the world to refuse his magnanimous gesture she knew if she didn't sit down soon she would collapse in an undignified heap on the expensive carpets. 'It would appear Lectron have a little problem.' The phrasing was pointed and she could almost see Mr Ashton subside a little further into his enormous chair. 'I was promised an English assistant at this point in the proceedings,' Melik continued smoothly, his dark face expressionless. 'A Beryl Swinton, Mrs Jones's deputy?'

Louisa opened her mouth to speak and then closed it again. She knew her voice would come out as a breathless squeak and she just wouldn't give him the satisfaction. She nodded instead as though it were all known to her.

'Unfortunately Mr Ashton informs me that the lady has been rushed into hospital in England, appendix. . .' He let his voice fade away to savour the growing alarm in Louisa's huge brown eyes and, after a long moment when no one spoke, rose in one fluid animal-like movement to stand in front of the deep arched window, the late afternoon sunlight picking up a dark sheen of blue on the strong, virile black hair.

When the gold gaze turned back to her the beautiful eyes were remote and very cold. 'How can we surmount this problem, Miss Collins?' He smiled humourlessly. 'This lady was designated to work closely with me, you understand, and I do not like delays; indeed, there have even been those who have called me an impatient man.' The sardonic face was a closed mask and she had no idea of what he was thinking. 'I need a member of the English team who knows all the part numbers, the numbering systems, the method of working, who understands that there are high quality standards that *must* be maintained, and who will interface with me and transpose my requirements into the English style of working with no hesitation and implicit obedience. Mrs Jones assures me that you are such an individual. Is she right?'

For the last few minutes she had been mentally preparing herself for the death-blow when it came but, even so, hearing it put into words was beyond her wildest fears. Even in normal circumstances to work closely with this man would be like riding a giant roller-coaster that was out of control, breathtakingly terrifying and utterly exhausting. But in view of what had gone before. . . She turned to Mrs Jones quickly.

'But Sandra?' She was gabbling but she couldn't help it. 'Or Peter or Michael? Any of those could do it, I'm sure. I don't see ——'

'Miss Collins!' Mrs Jones's scandalised expression confirmed she had overstepped the mark by several hundred yards.

'You do not want the post, Miss Collins?' Melik's voice was smoothly reasonable. 'Too much responsibility perhaps?' He'd trapped her! As she turned from Mr Ashton's and Mrs Jones's barely concealed annoyance to face the heavy-lidded gaze a full realisation of the impossible position he'd put her in washed over Louisa in a hot wave. If she refused the opportunity after it had been offered to her she could forget promotion where Lectron was concerned, besides which the firm had been good to her, she had to admit it. Apart from the excellent monthly salary and steady promotions over the last six years the powers-that-be had given her two months' leave without question when Oliver—— She caught her breath painfully. And then this Turkish trip. The rest of the firm had been green with envy at the favoured few. Yes, she owed them, and what was Melik Haman after all? Just a man like any other. She wouldn't let him intimidate her; Oliver would have expected her to stand her ground.

'Sandra is excellent at her work but there are other requirements to this assignment, Miss Collins,' Mrs Jones said crisply into the silence. Louisa knew immediately what she meant. Sandra would be all out for a romantic interlude, which could prove embarrassing, whereas she. . . She could be relied upon to give no thought to a dalliance in that area and all her loyalties would be exclusively Lectron's. But the overwhelming factor in Mr Ashton's and Mrs Jones's eyes was that Melik Haman had decided on her. Nothing else mattered. It was as simple as that.

'Well, Miss Collins?' Melik's voice was silky smooth and perfectly pitched but she knew from the narrowing of the hooded eyes that he had sensed her capitulation. He could smell it, she was sure of it, like a big black panther that had settled on its prey and was sizing up its advantage. 'You feel it would be too much for you?'

'On the contrary, Mr Haman.' She smiled carefully as she answered, pleased her voice was steady and cool when her heart was pounding so violently that she was sure it must be visible. 'I would be pleased to accept such an interesting post and I'll do my best not to let you down in any way.'

'Oh, you will not let me down, Miss Collins.' As the hard, glittering eyes swept over her upturned face again they lingered on the wide, soft mouth for a moment before meeting her gaze. 'I do not allow such things to happen.' It was said with such arrogance and regal disregard for her own feelings of human frailty that for a moment she was speechless, and then she responded as she had responded to all the challenges, good and bad, in her twenty-eight years of life — head-on, with chin held high and spirit fighting.

Why, you're just a bully, Melik Haman, she thought furiously as sheer anger replaced all other emotion and turned her eyes into black chips. A nasty, arrogant, spoilt bully who thinks he's holding all the aces and hasn't hesitated to use them.

Something of what she was feeling must have been clear to the others because she found herself ushered into the main office by a determined and red-faced Mrs Jones before she could say another word and with her feet hardly touching the ground.

'I'll explain everything later, Miss Collins.' Mrs Jones patted her arm in what could almost have been termed a maternal gesture. 'You'll get on with him all right after a time, you're a good girl.' She had disappeared back into the inner sanctum before Louisa could reply, and as she stood, somewhat dazed by the force of her emotions and the suddenness of it all, Sandra noticed her arrival and called urgently from her place at her desk.

As she reached her friend's side she was aware that even little Dephni, normally the most studious of the Lectron employees, had raised interested eyes to her face and Sandra was positively exploding with curiosity. 'Dephni says that's Melik Haman, the all-wise and powerful one,' Sandra said with a lack of respect that caused the little Turkish girl to look at her with horror. 'What did he want? He can have anything, anything at all from me. . .' She rolled her eyes at Dephni with such lewdness that Louisa could have smiled if the circumstances had been different. The small Turkish girl had been brought up strictly by fervent Muslim parents and was in turns fascinated and appalled by Sandra's mischief-making.

'I'm to work with him for a time, that's all,' Louisa said quietly. 'Apparently Beryl was going to come out but she's in hospital with appendix trouble.'

'That's all!' Sandra's shriek caused more than a few heads to turn in their direction and as she lowered her voice a few octaves her eyes were frankly envious.

'You lucky dog! You lucky, *lucky* dog. So many goodies wrapped up in one neat parcel!'

'It's just a job, Sandra.' Louisa sat down at her desk. 'It might not even work out,' she finished flatly.

'Just a job? How can you say that?' Sandra leant forward conspiratorially. 'Come on, Lou, you've got to admit he's something else. You can't tell me he doesn't make the old heart beat just a bit faster!'

Louisa thought again of the cold, hard arrogance, the strong, overpoweringly male body and cruel, handsome face, and unbeknown to her an expression of distaste curled her lip. Oliver had been slim, fair and with a boyish charm that had made him almost pretty, his warm, caring personality shining out of mild blue eyes that had rarely darkened in anger. He had been good to her, so good. . .

'I can see that you find him attractive, Sandra,' Louisa said slowly, her eyes looking inward and missing the dawning horror colouring her friend's face, 'but I can honestly say that if Melik Haman were the last man on earth I wouldn't want him. He does nothing for me, absolutely nothing.'

'Well, now that we have established that, Miss Collins, perhaps you would join me for a meal to formalise arrangements?' The deep, silky voice behind her froze her mind and body and for a moment she knew what it was to be totally paralysed with shock. As she slowly turned and raised her eyes upwards she saw his face was quite expressionless, his eyes frosted gold and his mouth unsmiling.

She thought about bluffing things out for a split second and then realised the futility of such action. She had been terribly rude and in front of two of his employees to boot; Sandra and Dephni were sitting in a frozen tableau as though someone had waved a wand and stopped the passage of time, and from the look on Dephni's face when the ice melted she would burst into tears.

'I'm sorry, Mr Haman,' she said quietly as the colour staining her cheeks rose up into the dark gold of her hair, 'you weren't meant to hear that. It was in reply to something that had been said—something complimentary,' she added hastily.

'Quite so.' The tawny gaze flicked over Sandra's and Dephni's stunned faces and for a moment she thought she saw a faint smile touch the cold mouth. 'Shall we go?'

'Go?' Louisa stared at him stupidly. What was he going to do? Incarcerate her in a dungeon somewhere?

'For lunch.' The dark voice was smoothly patient. 'I suggested to Mr Ashton that the final arrangements would be best concluded in an informal atmosphere to put you at your ease.'

'You did?' She glanced behind him at the firmly closed door of Mr Ashton's office. 'Where is he?'

'Otherwise engaged.' The narrowed eyes dared her to complain. 'And now if you're ready? We do have quite a lot to discuss. . .don't we, Miss Collins?' It was really a statement, not a question, and there was a wealth of meaning in the apparently innocent words.

Sandra handed her her shoulder-bag without speaking and Louisa took it in the same way. This was awful, terrible, and she had the uncomfortable feeling she had brought it all on herself. What on earth was he going to say to her when they were alone?

As Melik took her elbow in a firm grip and raised her to her feet she was conscious of his closeness, the clean male smell that emanated from his tanned skin, a mixture of delicious aftershave and sun-warmed flesh, but most of all the heat that his fingers induced. They were making the barest contact with her skin as they walked towards the door, his touch guiding rather than possessive, yet it seemed as though the contact was burning her and she could feel the fire spreading out in ripples over her skin. She didn't dare look at him as they left the office and began to walk down the massive stone steps towards the foyer, but she had never been so aware of another human being in her life.

'Calm down, Miss Louisa Collins.' The murmur in her ear was just audible to the two of them alone, and almost in the same breath Melik smiled and nodded to two young office girls walking up the stairs which had the effect of one of them losing her grip on the big box of files she was carrying, and almost falling to her knees in an effort to retrieve them before they cascaded away. Louisa had the sudden feeling that the little incident was indicative of the effect Melik normally had on women.

'You're enjoying this, aren't you?' she hissed quietly without looking to right or left and the answering chuckle at her side made her grate her teeth in impotent anger.

'You'll never know how much, my little tigress,' the hateful voice replied. 'The moment when you walked into that office was everything I had hoped for and more.'

'You're a, a. . .' She was spluttering with rage again and as she turned to him to vent her anger she found the feline eyes were looking straight at her, a hardness in their depths that suggested he was not quite so amused with the situation as he would like her to believe.

'Don't try and label me, Louisa.' They had reached the foyer now and she was painfully conscious of the little stir Melik's arrival caused, especially among the female population, although he seemed totally unaware of the veiled and not so veiled glances in his direction.

His ego must be jumbo size, she thought balefully as she glared at one particular well endowed redhead whose bust size had suddenly grown a few inches as she moved her body into the best possible stance for attracting Melik's attention. How could these women be so obvious?

'We are going to eat lunch now, Louisa.' He came to a halt just before the revolving doors and lifted her chin to raise her face to his as he looked down at her grimly. 'You will be well behaved and submissive as befits a newly hired secretary being taken out for a meal by her boss.' She was vitally conscious of his great height as he towered over her, the light musky perfume that drifted off his skin sending her senses into hyperdrive. 'Do you understand me?'

He gave her no chance to reply, ushering her out into the hot, busy, noisy street whereupon a chauffeur-driven Mercedes appeared like magic at their side and she found herself installed in its air-conditioned depths without being aware of how she got there.

'That is better. It is more restful when you are quiet.' His voice was lazy as he stretched out his long legs at her side after issuing orders in rapid Turkish to the uniformed driver. She glared at him but didn't answer, letting her heart slow down in time with her breathing as she took a few long hidden breaths.

The car was magnificent. In spite of her misgivings Louisa found the drive through the crowded, colourful streets with the vast cupola of St Sophia dominating the skyline as it had for the last one thousand, four hundred years luxuriously comfortable. She normally travelled in dolmuşes, one of Istanbul's shared taxis, with Sandra and a few other English personnel on the daily journey to and from work, but although cheaper than conventional taxis the vast majority of dolmuşes were American 55 Chevys and the like and when crowded to capacity did not make for a restful or relaxing homecoming in the hot, fume-laden air. The sign on most of the dashboards, 'Masallah', which roughly translated meant 'May God protect you', she always found particularly apt after a journey on the crazily crowded streets, where the drivers always seemed to see someone they knew, hanging out of the window to shout greetings and waving as they careered madly past.

'I am trying to work out if you are real.' The cool, deep voice was thoughtful.

'If I'm real?' She stared at him in surprise. They had been travelling for a few minutes in an uncomfortable silence that Louisa had found herself unable to break. She had been aware of his eyes on her for the last few moments but had kept her face turned to the window, her profile calm even as her heart thudded in her chest.

'Are you as totally unaware of your beauty as you seem?' he asked slowly. 'You do not touch your hair, glance in a mirror to check your make-up. . .' He eyed her musingly. 'Have I found that rare pearl? A beautiful woman without vanity?'

'I don't have the faintest idea what you are talking about,' she said stiffly as fire flooded into her cheeks.

'And this.' He touched the hot, silky skin lightly. 'You are. . .how old?'

'Twenty-eight.' Her voice was flat.

'Twenty-eight and yet you still blush so prettily,' he drawled mockingly. 'It's most attractive, but then, maybe you know this? Maybe it is all a clever strategy to attract even as you rebuff?'

'Don't flatter yourself.' Her voice was icy and as she turned to face him her eyes were flashing sparks.

'I rarely do.' His voice was dry. 'I find there are many people who are only too ready to perform that service for me. But not you.' Now his gaze sharpened. 'I have to give you that, not you.'

'Maybe I think you are conceited enough already?' She expected him to be insulted, angry, but the gold eyes crinkled with laughter.

'The male ego is a fragile piece of equipment, my little tigress; have pity.'

'I don't think yours is at risk,' she said cynically. 'Not with your wealth and. . .passable good looks.'

He bowed his head ironically. 'Careful, Louisa, don't be too enthusiastic. And you are quite right — mine is not at risk from your opinion or anyone else's, but not on account of my physical appearance or solvency.'

'No?' She raised her eyebrows disbelievingly.

'No.' His voice was quiet now and deep, his eyes sombre. 'I am thirty-seven years of age and due to the many circumstances of my life which I will not bore you with today I have the dubious blessing of knowing myself — my weaknesses, my strengths, the good, the bad. . .' His gaze wandered up to her hair and then back to the wide brown eyes. 'I say a dubious blessing because once a man or woman has reached that stage in life, and some never do, it can be a dangerous awareness. The human spirit needs a little uncertainty, a little vulnerability to keep it soft, open, alive.'

'And yours hasn't got that?' she asked almost in a

whisper, sensing this compelling man was speaking of things he normally didn't reveal.

He gazed for a long moment into the soft velvet darkness of her eyes and then, before she had time to react, his lips were on hers, not in a fleeting sigh but in a hard, hungry kiss that sent her senses spinning into another world where touch and sensation were the only things that mattered.

She was free again even as the strange feeling of every bone melting in her body registered on her stunned mind, and as he sank back into his seat it was as though a great beautiful cat had leashed its claws for a moment's respite, each muscle tensed and hard in anticipation.

'I had thought not.' His mouth twisted as he smiled to himself. 'But maybe. . .' The flecked eyes settled on her face and became withdrawn, remote. 'Who really knows themself, after all?' he said lightly. 'Do you?'

'Me?' She stared at him in confusion. 'I think I do. . . No, I don't. . . Oh, I don't know.' Her lips were burning from the brief contact with his hard, firm mouth and she suddenly felt a stab of blazing anger that she was reduced to a quivering wreck whereas he. . . He was cool and controlled and seemed to be finding the whole situation slightly amusing. And why shouldn't he? she thought with sickening honesty. He was immensely wealthy, dangerously powerful and she doubted if the word 'failure' had ever featured in his vocabulary, be it in regard to women or the business world in which he lived. She had sparked his jaded palate by the moves she had made, in all innocence, to avoid him. And that had placed her in a dangerous and vulnerable position. She looked again at the breathtakingly attractive face and hard, lean body and drew a deep, shuddering breath. She was going to have to be on her guard every moment around this man, *every single moment*.

CHAPTER THREE

'LOUISA?' She was brought out of her frightening reverie abruptly as Melik's cool voice claimed her attention.

'Oh, I'm sorry?' She realised too late he had spoken and she hadn't heard a word.

'I don't usually have to repeat myself when I am in female company,' he said silkily, 'but I am beginning to realise that "usual" is not a word that applies to you.'

'No?' She stared him full in the face, her eyes stormy.

'No. I haven't had a woman bolt on me before either,' he drawled mockingly. His expression was unchanging but despite the cool amusement Louisa could sense something, something dark and hard under the smiling mask. 'You are somewhat refreshing.'

'I'm so glad you approve,' she said tightly, and now he laughed outright, his flecked eyes narrowing.

'I didn't say I approved,' he corrected softly. 'In fact you put me to a great deal of time and trouble trying to find you and all the time you were safely caught in my net without my even knowing. Fate was laughing at both of us, my little tigress.'

'Please stop calling me that,' she snapped ungraciously as she tried to master her body's betrayal at his closeness. 'And I am most certainly *not* yours!'

'Then whose?' The reply had been whip-sharp. 'Was there — *is* there a man foolish enough in England to let you go for twelve months?'

'That's none of your business,' she said hotly.

'Yes, it is.' The hard ruthlessness he had displayed in the office was suddenly very much in evidence. 'We are going to be working very closely together over the next few weeks and you know as well as I do that they are crucial to this project's success. I do not need someone swooning over love-letters from England or making long telephone calls of a personal nature, so again I ask. . .' He paused coldly. 'Is there anyone in England?'

She stared at him helplessly, hating his questions, hating *him*, hating the vibrant life that was evident in every line of his lean, hard, uncaring body. How do you answer something like this? she asked herself desperately as her mind raced wildly. Yes, there was someone in England. . . The memories flashed in fleetingly. Oliver, the day she had first met him when he had capsized the small boat he was punting down the river by standing up to wave to her, a cheeky grin on his young face. When he had emerged from the brown water, dripping wet and disgustingly muddy, to collapse in a laughing heap on the bank, she had offered to run him back to his flat in her car for some dry clothes, and that had been the beginning. . .

He had been gentle and kind and protective, all the qualities she had looked for in her father and never found. Not that her father had been physically unkind, it was just that he had been so wrapped up in her mother, and she in him, that anyone else had merely stayed on the perimeter of their lives, even their own daughter. And she had grown to accept that she was unlovable, unwanted, her physical appearance counting for nothing to her in the face of their unintentional cruelty.

But Oliver had loved her. If that love had sometimes been a little dogmatic, a little dull, it hadn't mattered. He had been completely, wholly hers, she had known that from the first meeting, and the settling down of their relationship, the routine, the comfortableness. . . well, that happened to everyone, didn't it? That was life, the real world.

After twelve months they had set their engagement for the New Year, their wedding for the end of August, and a long September honeymoon somewhere hot. And then, three weeks before Christmas, Oliver had begun to feel tired, deathly tired, and a rare and virulent blood disorder was diagnosed. And within two months she had been left all alone again, unable really to take in that she would never see him again.

The last few weeks of his life she had been with him almost every minute; Lectron had given her the leave without quibbling and she would be eternally grateful for that precious time when she had been able to comfort, to reassure, to lie. . .

He had died believing he was going to get well and she felt no guilt about that. He wouldn't have been able to cope with the truth. But it had made it doubly hard for her.

And when he had left her a little bit of her soul had gone with him. She had weathered the feeling of loneliness since she was a little girl, her insecurity and lack of confidence making her outwardly self-sufficient and inwardly wary of any show of affection, but through Oliver new doors had beckoned, the promise of a life where there would be children, her own home, and most importantly of all where *she* would be the pivot of someone's life, loved and being able to give love. And when that had been so cruelly snatched away she had made the decision that never again would she open herself up to such devastating pain. And she wouldn't, ever. . . .

She raised her head and looked straight into the tawny green-flecked eyes, unaware that the play of emotions across her face had caused the man watching her so intently to catch his breath and wonder. . . 'No,' she said dully, her face wooden now, 'there is no one in England.'

The restaurant was close to the Topkapi Palace, the seat of the Ottoman sultans for three hundred years where power politics had mingled with the intrigues of the harem, and it was to this tiny walled city in miniature that Melik referred as they sat down at their table, his expression as bland and carefully friendly as it had been since their conversation in the car.

'You haven't been there yet?' he asked incredulously as she shook her head to his question. 'And you have been three weeks in Istanbul?' He shook his head slowly. 'I do not believe it.'

'There's hardly been any free time at all,' she said defensively, 'and Mrs Jones keeps everyone's nose to the grindstone.'

'Nose to the grindstone?' His smile, the first she had seen of genuine, unaffected amusement uncoloured by cynicism or sensual overtones, brought her heart thumping into her throat. It transformed the handsome, intimidating face so completely that it made her bruised heart ache. 'This grindstone must be most uncomfortable,' he said seriously, his eyes laughing at her. 'In that case I feel you deserve an afternoon sightseeing, and where better to start than with the most fascinating palace of them all? We will eat and then stroll.'

'I can't do that!' She looked at him aghast. 'The office ——'

'I own the office,' he reminded her coolly, 'and believe me, Louisa, when we start work tomorrow you will feel you have earnt every minute of this respite. You are going to put in more hours, and more blood, sweat and tears over the next few weeks than even the formidable Mrs Jones could ask.'

'But ——'

'For goodness' sake, woman, you do not want to see the palace?' His voice was tight with irritation at her discomfiture, his accent suddenly very marked.

'Of course I do,' she answered back in the same tone, 'but not with ——' She stopped abruptly as the glittering gold gaze dared her to continue.

'Not with me?' he finished icily. 'Well, that is a cross you will have to bear.' He settled back in his seat as he spoke, the immaculate suit and beautiful silk shirt and tie he wore so casually bringing the waiters hovering around like bees sensing a honey-pot.

The restaurant had a first-class, international flavour and was situated just outside the Topkapi Palace walls on Sogukcesme Sok. Melik had commented that the whole street was reminiscent of New Orleans but not having been there she merely nodded quietly, her eyes widening at the prices on the menu.

It was as they finished the first course of *cacik*, a delicious mixture of yoghurt and chopped cucumbers, and the waiter had begun to fill a small side-table with an array of temptingly aromatic dishes for the main course, that Melik dropped his minor bombshell — a punishment, she felt immediately, for her earlier rejection of his company.

'You will not mind the travelling, I hope?' He smiled slowly as he gave her a long, calculating look that made her instantly alert.

'Travelling?' With a tremendous effort she kept her voice steady. 'Exactly what do you mean?'

'It's obvious, surely?' Melik's voice and face had assumed an innocent, open quality that caused Louisa's toes to curl in her high, open-toed sandals.

'I'm sorry.' She smiled as coolly as she could. 'You'll have to be more explicit.'

'I travel all over the country, Louisa; I actually have homes in the Black Sea region and the south-west, and then of course there are my frequent trips abroad, although I would not expect you to accompany me on those.' He smiled with gentle reasonableness. 'But you would find my château in France a particular delight.'

'Doubtless.' She eyed him coldly.

'I would, of course, need my English assistant with me at all times. I am not prepared to lose valuable time making unnecessary telephone calls and dictating letters into one of those infernal machines without seeing instant results. You understand?'

'Perfectly.' She glared at him angrily as the silent waiter replenished their half-full glasses of *misbag*, a white wine that tasted fruitily of the raisin grapes it was made from.

'Good.' He smiled smoothly. 'And now please enjoy your food. Have you tried the *cerkez tavugu* before?'

'Probably.' Her eyes were icy. 'I could answer that question in more detail if I knew what it was.'

'Chicken served in a thick sauce made from walnuts,' he said cheerily, quite unperturbed by her rage. 'It's delicious, trust me.' Her face answered him with such frankness that he was shaking with silent laughter as he served her a small portion from each of the side-dishes, explaining each mouthwatering spoonful as he did so. 'Puréed spinach, broad beans marinated in olive oil, fried aubergine slices with yoghurt, mussels stuffed with rice, pine nuts and currants, and, of course, pilaf rice. OK?'

She nodded slowly, aware that he had been careful to choose dishes that were not highly spiced and secretly grateful for his consideration. 'Thank you, it looks lovely,' she said quietly.

'Thank you, it looks lovely, *Melik*.' The gold eyes were broodingly intent. 'You have been very correct so far but I am sure you can relax just a little?'

'You are my boss,' she said quickly. 'It wouldn't be right to ——'

'Melik,' he said with a silky thread of steel running through his rich voice. 'In the office, out of it, wherever. . . Understand?'

'If you say so.' The blood was so hot in her cheeks that they actually hurt.

'Oh, I do.' In contrast he was relaxed, cool, and seemed to be thoroughly enjoying the meal. 'Now eat up and don't sulk; I find that the least attractive failing in the female sex.'

'I never sulk,' she said hotly, 'never.'

'Is that so?' He leant forward suddenly, his face a breath away as his eyes travelled slumberously over her flashing eyes and angry mouth. 'And the other little tricks and fancies that a woman uses to get her own way? They are learnt from babyhood, especially when the female in question has more than her fair share of beauty like you. I would imagine that you had the men in your household twisted round your delightful little finger.'

'There was only my father,' she said tightly as the pain bit deep, 'and you are quite wrong.' She tried with all her might to stop even a shred of anguish filtering through in her voice but the hard face sharpened suddenly, his eyes narrowing and then widening as he shook his head.

'I seem to have hit a nerve; I apologise, I have no wish to hurt you.'

'You couldn't.' Her smile was brittle and she finished the glass of wine in one gulp without being aware of it, spearing a piece of chicken on her fork and tasting it quickly. 'Delicious; do you know how it's cooked?' The diversion was obvious but he was too much of a gentleman to ignore it, and the rest of the meal was conducted with banal conversation, the pace slow and unhurried as in most Turkish eating places.

She hated this man! Louisa's thoughts were quite at odds with her outward appearance. Hated, loathed, detested. . .there weren't enough adjectives in any language to describe how she felt about him. How dared he make his sweeping statements that were so cruel, so —— ? She forced her mind to stop its destructive cycle. He had asked for her to work with him, as a penance, a punishment, and so be it. Her eyes were cloudy and dark. But if he expected anything else he was in for a shock! And she was going to make that clear, crystal-clear, at the first opportunity!

As they finished the desert of *baklava*, a deliciously flaky pastry bulging with nuts in syrup, Louisa felt her stomach muscles begin to tense. She hadn't really tasted any of the meal—the weight of her thoughts had turned it to sawdust in her mouth — and now she had to spend the afternoon with him? It was monstrous. . .

'I have distressed you with my clumsy talk.' As her hand was taken in his she flinched back automatically, her eyes shooting up to his face.

'I'm perfectly all right,' she said stiffly.

His eyes had hardened at her withdrawal and now she saw he made a visible effort before speaking again. 'Louisa, you are very beautiful and I am appreciative of such loveliness,' he said slowly. 'Can we not try to establish a relationship of harmony —— ?'

She interrupted him before he had time to finish, her eyes blazing with outrage. He thought a few soft words, a convenient carefully worded apology and she would fall into his arms in happy surrender? He was appreciative of loveliness? Well, bully for him! He had said himself the days of the harem were over and there was no way, even for a minute, she was going to let him think she would be content to be one of the many who no doubt frequented his bed!

'I never mix business with pleasure, Mr Haman,' she said tightly, 'and I'm sure you would be the first to applaud such sentiments. I am good at my job and I will do my best to fulfil the duties I have been given, and of course I'm sure we'll work well together. That is all that's necessary, isn't it?'

He held her glance for a long, still moment and then nodded curtly. 'Quite.'

She felt an overwhelming misery swamp her for a few seconds at his hard voice and cold eyes, but pushed the weakness aside determinedly. It would be suicide to let him get under her skin.

As they emerged from the pleasant, air-conditioned restaurant into the busy street he took her arm in that proprietorial gesture she was beginning to know. In spite of her churning feelings she felt a moment of guilty pleasure at being held close to his side as several female heads swivelled round for a second and third look, but then the feel of his hard-muscled body next to hers caused the blood to sing through her veins and she took a deep, calming breath as they began to walk towards the Topkapi Palace. The response of her body to his shocked her; she had never imagined such strong physical attraction was possible. Oliver had never seemed particularly interested in that side of their relationship, content to wait until they got married to consummate their love, and before him she had never really had a serious boyfriend, just a few brief encounters where no more than a few hugs and kisses were involved. Oliver had surprised her with his easy contentment and lack of ardour, but it was only now that she realised, as the big, lean body at her side sent the strangest sensations flowing down into her limbs, that she had felt all along there was something wrong, that there ought to be more. The thought was a painful betrayal.

She wondered what this strange, passionate man at her side would say if she told him she had never had a lover. Laugh his head off, no doubt, her mind told her tersely. Twenty-eight years old and still a virgin? He wouldn't believe it.

'Do you have a flat in England, Louisa?' The tone was pleasantly conversational but she stiffened instinctively before forcing herself to relax. He was right; they were going to spend a great deal of time together over the next weeks and months, so it was ridiculous not to communicate naturally.

'I did have.' She smiled brightly. 'But it was rented

and the other three girls couldn't carry my share for a year and I couldn't afford to subsidise from here so they got someone else when I left.' He nodded. The answer seemed to please him although she couldn't imagine why.

'And your family?'

This time she was prepared. 'My parents live in Sussex and I am an only child,' she said quietly. 'I left home for college at eighteen and haven't lived with them since.' She continued quickly before he could speak. 'And you? Do your parents live close by?'

'My father died several years ago, a heart attack.' He looked down at her slowly. 'He was Turkish and my mother is French so she decided to go back to France to live with her sister who was also widowed at about the same time. They are happily established in a château a few miles from mine where they argue all day long about anything and everything.' There was a look on his face that touched a chord deep inside her; in spite of his words it was clear that he loved his mother very much. 'They are a pair of quite dreadfully irascible old ladies but they keep each other young.'

'Have you any brothers or sisters?' she asked with a curiosity that surprised her.

'No.' He smiled softly. 'I was what you may call a late arrival. I understand my parents had given up hope of ever having a child and then I arrived.'

'You must have been spoilt.' She was quite unaware of the note of raw envy in her voice and unconscious of the perceptive glance he shot at her from under heavy brows.

'Undoubtedly, but then Turkish children often are, although only, in my opinion, in the very best way.

Children are precious here; I wish it were so in more countries.'

'Yes.' She bit her lip till it hurt. Why was any conversation with this man guaranteed to hurt?

The Topkapi Palace was everything she had imagined and much, much more. Behind the Imperial Gate the four courts stretched majestically rich with the treasures of a bright lost age when money had been no object to the favoured few, and the sultans had had absolute and unquestioning power.

Although the First Court with its beautiful concert hall, the Second with a museum holding exquisitely delicate Chinese and Japanese porcelain and the others with the four-roomed Treasury holding regal pre-eminence were breathtakingly lovely, it was the Harem that drew Louisa's complete fascination.

The secluded quarters of the wives and concubines of the Sultan, shaded by cypresses and plane trees, fired her imagination vividly, and as they walked through the gates where only the Sultan himself had been allowed to ride on horseback, even his viziers being forced to walk, she felt a strange feeling trickle down her spine that was magnified as she glanced up to find Melik's brilliant gold gaze tight on her face. 'Just less than a hundred years ago a beautiful English girl with pale, honey-coloured skin and hair the colour of corn would not have been free to walk through these gates of her own free will.' His eyes lingered for a moment on the tiny curling whisps that had escaped the severe knot and wandered closer to her face, and then he moved almost sharply, pulling her tighter into his side and looking straight ahead. 'You would have been brought here by the chief eunuchs, probably in chains and with your hair falling in glorious abandonment about your bare shoulders, terrified, frightened and all alone. They would have dragged you to the quarters of the Black Eunuch, who held the highest office of all, being the adviser and confidant of the Sultan, and his black eyes would have lit up at the sight of such a prize for his master.'

She wanted to stop the sensual pictures he was painting in her mind but her power of speech, indeed her very thoughts, were subjugated in fascinated compliance.

'He would have ordered that you be treated as a queen, the very best of perfumes, lotions being used to anoint your body for painstakingly long weeks until your hair and skin were the texture of pure silk and your body was ripe for surrender. Then you would be clothed in veils, each one transparent and soft, allowing a brief glimpse of the beauty beneath, and he would take you to his master, throwing you at the Sultan's feet before kneeling with his head touching the floor as he paid homage to the all-powerful and mighty one. And then. . .'

His voice died away and Louisa felt her eyes being raised to his as though she were drugged. 'And then?'

'The Sultan would smile at such a treasure, such a priceless treasure, and the Black Eunuch would know that he had succeeded, that his position was more secure than it had ever been because he would have been the one to give his master the ultimate prize, the favourite.'

The slow warm ache that had taken hold of her limbs, turning them to water, made Louisa glad of Melik's arm holding her so tightly, even as the burning tawny gaze seemed to sear into her brain.

'The Eunuch would leave and at a glance from their

master's commanding face the other slaves would melt away until at last it was just you and him. He would ask to see the beauty that he could only glimpse at and you would refuse, shrinking back against the floor as he left his jewel-studded throne to stand over you, magnificent and dark in his flowing robes of purple and black, the jewels flashing on his brown hands. He would be gentle where you expected force, considerate where you feared violence and ravishment, lifting you to your feet as he slowly unwound the floating veils from your trembling body until at last you would stand naked and shaking before him. He would coax you, use all the skills and vast sensual knowledge he possessed until you were compliant and submissive, trembling now not with fear but with a strange excitement that——'

'Stop it!' She swung away from him so violently that she nearly knocked a tiny Japanese man who was unfortunate enough to be passing at the time clear off his feet. 'That's enough; I don't want to hear any more.' She couldn't believe she was letting a man, a virtual stranger, affect her like this. What on earth was the matter with her? It must be the heat and this whole sensual experience of a place. The very air seemed to breathe a fleshly, voluptuous intimacy that made her flesh tingle.

Oliver. She summoned up the name as an unconscious talisman for protection. She must think of Oliver. It didn't occur to her until many weeks later that that instant was the first time she had ever forced herself to think of him.

She didn't fully appreciate the beauty of the Harem, recently lovingly restored, as she tried desperately to bring her wandering senses and aroused feelings under control. The vivid picture that Melik had so skilfully painted was there in the forefront of her mind and every tile, every room, was a vivid reminder. It horrified her, thrilled her, to her shame, and made her aware of dark emotions buried deep within her that she had never known existed and dared not acknowledge.

The principal royal apartments were quite magnificent and as they wandered through the audience chamber, bedroom, prince's quarters and the Pasha's mother's bedroom, where a personal slave girl had slept over the canopy of her four-poster bed, the full enormity of the Sultan's absolute power and authority washed over her again.

'The Sultan had up to two hundred concubines to attend to his needs,' Melik whispered softly in her ear as she paused in the exotic atmosphere to take in a particularly beautiful silk curtain hiding yet another quiet, slumberous room. 'A most fortunate man, wouldn't you say?'

She turned round quickly, her eyes sparking as they took in the lazy, confident smile and arrogantly male body. 'You agree with such a chauvinistic concept, then?' she asked tightly. 'I might have known.'

'You seem to have answered the question you asked me yourself,' he said coolly as his eyes fastened on her jutting chin and temper-flushed cheeks.

'You'd answer differently?' She stared at his handsome face aggressively. 'Well, would you?'

'Louisa, Louisa. . .' The unspoken amusement colouring his voice was more irritating than he would ever know, she thought furiously. 'All this contention, hostility, why?' The feline eyes narrowed thoughtfully.

'Why do you feel the need to oppose me so strongly, to be suspicious of everything I say?'

'I wasn't aware I did,' she said tightly. 'Maybe you mistake normal healthy disagreement for something else?'

'Maybe.' He was smiling openly now and she would have given the world to hit him, hard. 'One thing is for sure — the minute you were brought through the gates the Harem would never have been the same again.'

She glared at him without answering and his light chuckle brought the blood rushing to her cheeks. The nerve of the man! He was constantly provoking her with everything he said, every little comment, and all that talk about the Harem before. . . He had made love to her! Without even touching her he had made love to her. It was. . .it was *immoral*.

'Here's the car.' They had continued the tour in silence and once outside the palace grounds she saw the regal Mercedes with a stab of relief. 'You enjoyed your taste of culture?'

'Yes, thank you.' As Melik opened the door for her she almost collapsed inside the car. Enjoyed it? Well, that was one way of putting it.

'Good.' He settled back as before, strong legs outstretched in relaxed ease and one arm resting on the back of the seat, which brought physical contact precariously close. His whole body language spoke of perfect contentment and peace with his surroundings whereas she. . . She was going mad, she thought grimly as the powerful car drew out into the honking, chaotic traffic.

'The Blue Mosque next, I think, another day.'

'Another day?' Her head snapped round to his immediately.

'It should not be missed,' he continued silkily. 'One cannot describe the vast beauty of its interior, the two hundred windows, exquisite coloured stencilling, the sheer majesty of the place. No visit to Istanbul is complete without seeing the Blue Mosque; it is disgraceful you haven't been yet. I——'

'I think I'm going to be too busy over the next few weeks to go sightseeing,' she said stiffly, cutting into his deep voice determinedly. 'Besides which I think it would be most unwise to associate on a social level with you or anyone else at the office. People talk. . .' Her voice dwindled away as something dangerous leapt into the gold slits watching her so closely.

'Do they?' he asked coldly. 'And what do these people say when they talk?'

'You know what I mean,' she snapped quickly. 'It's all right for you; your reputation——' She stopped abruptly, aware that what she had been about to say was neither tactful nor polite.

'My reputation?' Now he was really angry; she saw it in the dark flare of red on the high cheekbones and the flaring of the straight nose. 'Yes? Please continue.'

'Well, it's different for a man,' she said tightly, throwing caution to the wind. 'It's all hail and well met, isn't it? Back-slapping and "you're a fine stud" type of thing. No one would think any the worse of you if they thought that we. . .that you. . .' The ice in his eyes was making her flounder. 'Whereas I would be put in quite a different category.'

'A fine stud?' The note in his voice would have been comical if the look on his face hadn't been so terrifying. 'Believe me, if anyone, male or female, ever made the mistake of referring to me as a stud, fine or otherwise, they would live to regret it.' He eyed her furiously. 'I

can't believe that in this day and age you still hold such
outdated views.'

'Outdated views?' Now it was her turn to look
amazed. 'What sort of cloud-cuckoo-land are you living
in anyway? Maybe the jet-set hold different values
from everyone else, as the tabloids would have us
believe, but I can assure you that in the normal
everyday world in which *I* inhabit a girl getting over-
friendly with her boss is not the best reference I know.'

'Jet-set?' The flared nostrils twitched. 'Now who is
labelling whom?'

'I'm not arguing with you, Mr Haman,' she said
faintly as the knowledge that she was losing ground
began to dawn on her. 'The meal was lovely and I very
much appreciated your kind invitation to show me a
little of what Istanbul holds, but that's as far as it's
going. OK?'

'The hell it's OK!' They had just passed a magnificent
mosque, gold and silver in the evening sunlight, and as
a small dusty square surrounded by ancient houses and
quaint shops lit a spark of recognition in her she
realised she was nearly home. 'What do you think I
am, anyway? Some kind of rapacious animal, for crying
out loud?'

'Not at all.' As the car drew up with a flourish
outside the apartment block she felt a rush of relief
that was indescribable.

'Well, everything you've done and said so far is
making you a liar, Miss Collins.' The light had died
swiftly and now she could only just see his face in the
dancing shadows inside the car. 'And I am very
tempted to give you exactly what you expect from me
to teach you the lesson you deserve.'

'You just try it and——'

He moved sinuously against her in one fluid cat-like movement that had her caught under his body as securely as if she were in the chains he had spoken of earlier, her hands caught in his iron grasp and his mouth locked on to hers in a kiss that brought shocking tension to every part of her body. The hard contours of his male shape were pressed into her soft curves in a perfect male-female jigsaw that had the blood flowing hot in her veins as she recognised the arousal he was making no effort to hide, and after a few moments, as a rush of searingly hot pleasure had her horrified at her body's betrayal, she felt the potency of his desire melting her resistance.

This was how a man could make you feel, then? Lost in an excitement that had no reason to it, no control?

He was neither rough nor violent, his mouth warm and sensual as it did its devastating work of cutting through her defences and turning her soft and melting beneath his skilful lovemaking until at last he released her hands, knowing she was his captive, that the trembling, fluttering female shape beneath his was wholly subjugated.

Her throat was his now, thrown back and defenceless as she lay half swooning in his arms, and as he lightly touched his lips to the frantic pulse beating there she moaned softly, unable to think, to care. . . This was everything she had dreamed about as a young starry-eyed girl when she had read her first romance, and so much more besides. It couldn't be real. *He* couldn't be real. A glimmer of uneasiness penetrated the stupor his lovemaking had caused, making itself felt now that his hands and mouth had stopped their devastating work. She opened dazed eyes to see his face an inch from her own, and strangely it didn't hold the cynical satisfaction she had expected.

'And *I* was teaching *you* the lesson?' His voice was faintly incredulous. 'How many people live under your skin, Louisa?'

The searing embarrassment turned her skin scarlet as she struggled upwards and out of his hold, backing into a corner of the car as though she were a tiny animal trying to hide. The dark little street in which the apartment block was situated was deserted but she felt as though the very walls had eyes, and although the linen screen in front of the glass that separated the driver from the passengers was very firmly anchored in place she felt exposed, vulnerable and horribly mortified.

'Don't look like that.' As Melik reached out for her she shrank still further from him and immediately his hand dropped back. 'What happened between us. . .' He shook his head slowly. 'It was as much a surprise to me as it was to you, I promise. I didn't expect —' He stopped abruptly.

'Please let me go.' She was opening the door as she spoke, fumbling with the handle, and as he made to follow her she knew her voice was rising but couldn't control the pain any longer. 'Leave me alone.' She stared at him wild-eyed, unaware that her hair had come loose in the close embrace and was framing her head and shoulders in a halo of shining golden curls that brought a burning darkness into the eyes watching her. 'You must leave me alone. I can't have this, I can't stand it. . .' Her voice broke on a sob and then she was gone, running into the building as though the devil himself were after her and not stopping until she burst into the flat, desperately relieved to find she was alone as Sandra had not returned yet.

He must think she was mad! After long, strained, painful minutes of staring into nothing she had forced herself to fix a cup of coffee in the tiny kitchen, more to give her hands something to do and stop the shaking in her limbs than anything else, and now, as the hot liquid calmed her mind, she found herself red with humiliation. Mad, deranged. . . She shut her eyes tightly in embarrassment. First of all running like a startled rabbit in the Bazaar and now this. Why couldn't she have handled it all differently, smoothly, coolly, maintaining a sedate distance at the same time as giving no offence? Because she wasn't the sort of woman he thought she was. The thought came with a sickening jolt. He was looking for a pleasant diversion for a short time with a willing partner who knew the score and wanted it as much as he did. That was the way men like him worked. Rich, handsome, spoilt, masterful men who had the world at their fingertips. And she couldn't handle it.

She rocked to and fro on the high stool in front of the minute breakfast-bar. She would tell Mrs Jones she had to go back to England tomorrow. Strangely the thought brought no comfort, only fresh pain. She would go home, find a new job, a new flat, and try to pick up the pieces of her life which the last twelve months had smashed into tiny fragments. Sudden tears were hot and gritty behind her closed eyelids and she moaned softly into the silence. In all the agonising time with Oliver and the harrowingly painful months after he had died she had never, ever felt such savagely overwhelming hopelessness, and that realisation, along with the events of the day, seemed the final betrayal to her memory of him. It was the key that unlocked the flood of tears that had her eventually crawling into bed, weary and heartsore, to fall into a deep, dreamless sleep until morning.

CHAPTER FOUR

'THAT last set of part numbers? Have those been checked, Louisa?'

'Yes, and the shipment received this morning too. Do you want me to fax the part number of that new processor chip through to England tonight?'

'Please.' Melik nodded abstractedly and Louisa smiled to herself quietly. The last two months had been a revelation on how much work one man could consume by the hour, and she had nearly missed the excitement, the utter absorption of working with such a razor-sharp, blindingly intelligent mind.

When she had arrived at the office that morning two months ago after her visit to the Topkapi Palace with Melik the day before she had been determined to leave Turkey as soon as possible. And he had been waiting for her, whisking her into his office before she'd even had a chance to open her mouth and sitting her in a chair as he had begun to talk at her. And it had been talking *at* her, she remembered with a wry smile.

'Where's the letter?' He had eyed her intimidatingly. 'The resignation letter?'

'In my bag.' She had been too raw and tired to resist.

'Rip it up.' He had uncoiled from his position on the side of the desk and begun to pace the floor, talking in quiet clipped tones as he'd outlined his plans for the next few weeks. 'Total business, Louisa, I promise, nothing else.' He'd glanced once at her swollen, mauve-stained eyes before continuing the pacing. 'I apologise for last night; I take utter and absolute blame, of course. For what it's worth I have never instigated an office liaison in my life before, I would like you to believe that.' She hadn't nodded or replied, her great eyes fixed on his dark face as he'd prowled round the small room. 'I want you to stay; it would mean the loss of your job here and possibly at Lectron in England if you left and it is not necessary. We can work well together; I need someone who is prepared to put in long hours almost constantly and frankly from what I've seen of the rest of the contingent you stick out like a sore thumb.' She hadn't, even then, feeling as empty as she did, liked the simile. 'We have got off to a bad start but it is not irretrievable and now I feel we both know where we stand. Well?' The piercing eyes had suddenly fixed on her face. 'Are you going to run or stay here and do the job that Lectron is expecting of you?'

She had recognised the clever psychology even then, although she was going to become more familiar with it in the weeks ahead, when she watched, amazed, as he manipulated situations and people to his will with very little effort, but his words had hit a raw spot. Lectron *had* supported her unhesitatingly when she had needed it, even if one could argue that she had always been the model employee and excellent at her job, and she hadn't liked the idea of letting them down.

'I'll stay.' Her voice had been wooden. 'At least for the time being.'

The somewhat one-sided conversation with Melik in absolute control had set the tone for the following weeks. Their working relationship had been one of cool efficiency interlaced with hectic and exhausting panics at least once a day, and gradually Louisa had come to accept that he had forgotten the brief and strange passion he had had for her and now regarded her as a necessary part of the office equipment without which the project couldn't function properly, and yet. . .

She glanced under her eyelashes at him now as he straightened from his sitting position behind the huge desk and stretched wearily. There were times, just now and then, when she caught him looking at her in a certain way, a dark intensity colouring the golden eyes bronze, but immediately he registered her glance a shutter would snap down over the beautiful eyes and he would become the remote professional again, cool, calm and very much in command. And she would be left thinking it was all in her imagination.

He was a vitally complex man, that much she had learnt. Fiercely proud, unbearably authoritative, ruthless to the point of cruelty at times when faced with any inefficiency or laziness, and yet he was harder on himself than anyone, working far into the night when everyone else had gone and arriving long before dawn if the situation commanded it.

He was as proud of his French heritage as of his Turkish, fluent in six languages, undeniably cosmopolitan in his outlook and morals, and yet. . . She remembered the day he had told her he could trace his Turkish ancestry back to Suleyman the Magnificent, the greatest of all the Ottoman sultans. He had been all Turkish then. And his women! She shut her eyes for a moment. If all the rumours and whispered office hearsay were true he had his own version of the harem in modern-day Turkey, although where he found the time she would never know!

'Are you tired?' His voice brought her eyes snapping

open to see him leaning back in his big leather chair, hands behind his head, his shirt stretched tight over the broad masculine chest. Her breathing quickened before she had time to control it.

'A little.' She smiled carefully and forced her eyes to move to a point just over his left shoulder. 'It's been a long day.'

'One of many.' He smiled slowly. 'And tonight I think we can afford to indulge ourselves a little with a reward for hard endeavour. Yes?'

'A reward?' she asked cautiously. The only reward she wanted was to relax for an hour in a hot bath with maybe a glass of wine and a good book, followed by eight hours of uninterrupted sleep. It took that long to prepare the armour in mind and body for the close proximity with him each day.

'You'll need your jacket.' He nodded at the light wool thigh-length coat on the antique coat-rack in a corner of the room. 'The nights are getting cooler.' She eyed him without replying. This time last month the weather had been a comfortable seventy degrees most days but with the onset of November the temperature had fallen and now, three weeks through the month, a cooler fifty-seven had been recorded. Not bad by English standards but after the fierce, unrelenting heat of the summer months the change here was striking.

'Melik, I don't think this is a good idea.' She faced him squarely without reaching for her jacket.

'You don't eat?' he asked with simulated surprise, glancing down her slim shape consideringly. 'Well, I do and I'm starving.'

'You know what I mean——'

'Don't argue, Louisa.' The tone was soft and quiet and shut off her voice more effectively than any force.

'We are going for a bite to eat, that is all, OK?' She opened her mouth to speak and he silenced her with an upraised hand. 'Say, Yes, Melik,' he ordered softly.

'But——'

'Yes, Melik.' There was a faint thread of steel in the silky tones now and she knew defeat when she heard it.

'OK, but I can't be late; Sandra will send out a search party,' she said lightly as she turned for her coat, aiming for a cool, friendly approach to offset the sudden tension.

As she followed him out of the deserted building into the noisy, crowded street her eyes automatically skimmed along the kerb for Melik's distinctive Mercedes, her hand holding the English newspaper that one of the office staff always fetched each day from Divan Yolu, the main street in the Sultanahmet district.

'No car tonight.' As her eyes fastened on his face she saw he was smiling quietly. 'We can reach our destination by foot.'

'Can we?' As a thought occurred to her she frowned slightly, her eyes opening wider. 'Did you know we were going to do this, then?'

'It had crossed my mind.' His dark face was enigmatically distant and as she stared up at him he shook his head gently. 'You have the most transparent face of any female I know. Don't you ever try to hide your thoughts when they might be a little. . .uncomfortable for the recipient?'

'No.' She regarded him unsmilingly. 'Should I?'

'Perhaps not.' He shook his head again. 'It's just that your particular brand of honesty takes a little getting used to. I'm used to more co-operation from my women.'

'I don't doubt it,' she said tartly, 'but as I am not one of your women that comment is a little out of place.'

'*Touché*, child.' The sudden smile lit up the flecked eyes and she had to force herself not to smile back. He knew how devastating that smile was, she just knew it!

'I rather like this high horse of which you English speak,' he said softly, touching her flushed face with a thoughtful finger before taking her arm and putting it through his, drawing her comfortably into his side. 'Now, if we are going to negotiate the crowded pavements you will need a little protection.' As they walked along the uneven busy pavement she was glad he was concentrating on steering their path through the jumble of human bodies; it gave her time to get used to the feel of his hard, lean body next to hers and compose her face accordingly.

As they passed two small children splashing each other from one of the numerous fountains that could be found in every street and alley, in every courtyard, square and park, a particularly energetic splash sent a cascade of water showering over Melik's immaculate trousers in diamond droplets. Their apologies were immediate and profuse, and as she watched him bend down to reassure the infants, his eyes soft and his mouth smiling, she felt a sudden hard lurch to her heart that was almost painful. She had noticed this before, this gentleness with anything small and timid; even little Dephni in the office who held him in such awe always received a consideration that was lacking in his dealings with the more worldly-wise of his staff, and it produced feelings in her she would rather not acknowledge.

'Are you going to ask me where we are going?' As

they continued walking he glanced down at her after taking her arm in his again, turning off as he spoke into a long, narrow cobbled street that led downwards, away from the main throng.

'I suppose so.' She looked up at him and it was a mistake. His black hair had been ruffled by the salty wind and suddenly it was a much younger Melik who smiled down at her, younger and devastatingly attractive. The memory of that night in his car was, without warning, there in front of her and as she stumbled his arm tightened, drawing her even closer into his side.

'Steady.' He frowned down at their feet. 'These damn cobbles look picturesque enough but there are more broken ankles per square yard. . .'

He had felt so good. . . Her body seemed to have a life of its own, refusing her brain's command to ignore feelings that were best buried.

'Now, for dinner I can offer you giant mussels charcoal-grilled while you watch, the biggest peaches you'll ever see, from Bursa, nuts from the Black Sea. . .' As he had been talking they had arrived on the waterfront, somewhere she had always meant to visit but had not had the time for. She had heard of the culinary delights on its shores from the Turkish contingent in the office, and now she saw that they had not exaggerated the magic of the place. The quay was alive with rich colour and exotic smells, visitors and locals alike represented in the teeming, busy throng that swelled and moved like a flowing tide.

'Oh, it looks——' Her voice was cut off abruptly as she felt his fingers loosening the clip at the back of her head just a moment too late to stop her hair flying loose in a soft curling cloud around her face and shoulders, the tiny golden curls and soft waves gleaming in the light from the bright stalls and shops. 'Melik!' she protested weakly, her voice faltering as she looked up into the darkness of his eyes which wandered slowly over her hair and skin as if he were a thirsty man who had just been given his first taste of pure clean water. 'What did you do that for?'

'Because I wanted to,' he said thickly, 'and I have been more patient than you will ever know.'

'Melik——'

'No more words.' He cut off her protest abruptly by the simple expedient of placing his lips on hers for a fleeting second, the light touch sending ripples of awareness flooding into her limbs. 'We are going to eat.' He pointed to a glowing brazier a few feet away on which mussels, cubes of swordfish and other seafood lay gently sizzling in mouthwatering splendour. 'Or maybe shish kebab, corn-on-the-cob. . .?'

'Melik——'

'And do not say you are not hungry. You eat too little and work too hard. Has no one ever taken you in hand?'

It hurt. It shouldn't, because he had said it in total innocence, but nevertheless it hurt. He always hurt her. And she couldn't understand why. Couldn't understand why the remarks that would mean nothing from anyone else always seemed to find the vulnerable spot when spoken by him.

'You ought to be pleased because I work hard,' she said huskily. 'As my employer——'

'Oh, no.' He placed a finger on her lips, his eyes flashing. 'Tonight you are not keeping the barriers in place, my Louisa. I will not allow it.' There was a touch of the old arrogance in his tone and it made it easier to harden herself, to take a mental step backwards. She had to remember, *had* to remember that he was rich and powerful, that he was used to many different women, that his lifestyle was fast and furious and little incidents like this would mean nothing to him. Whereas she—— Her mind stopped and she didn't pursue the thought. Some people were meant to walk through life alone, she told herself fiercely as she watched him talking to a bearded stall-holder in long, flowing robes, pointing out some mussels for the heaped plates he was holding, and it was futile to fight against one's fate. She had already done that once with Oliver, and with catastrophic results.

All around the hot, spicy smells of the East were mingling with the vibrant, colourful waterfront, the occasional veiled woman clothed from head to foot in sombre black at variance with the gaily dressed tourists and majority of Turkish locals in casual jeans and jumpers. It was a melting-pot of a place and in other circumstances, in another world, she would have loved every minute, but now. . . She glanced across at Melik again to see that he was on his way back to her, the plates of food steaming gently. Now everything was too poignant, too strained, her nerves stretched as tight as piano strings.

'Here.' As he reached her side he flicked his head to a small wooden bench at the side of a wall. 'Eat and enjoy.' The smile he gave her was warm and soft and as he placed the plate of food in her hands his gaze lingered for a long moment on her face. 'It's eating with your fingers, I'm afraid.'

'I like that,' she said lightly. 'I think I'm quite uncivilised at heart.'

'Really?' As he joined her on the bench she was acutely aware of hard-muscled thighs under the thin material of his suit, even more so when he crossed one knee over the other and bit into a shish kebab with hard white teeth. 'Mmm, that's good.' He eyed her out of the corner of his eye. 'So you are a savage like me? Maybe there is hope for me yet, then.' As his teeth tore at the meat again her eyes followed in fascinated interest; he suddenly seemed quite unlike the awe-inspiring, ruthless businessman of the daytime hours who wielded such total and absolute power. She blinked as the golden gaze flicked over her face again. But she had to remember that like any dangerous animal he was at his most lethal when seemingly indolent and relaxed. She couldn't afford to be caught off guard again.

'Do you like it?' He waved a lazy hand at the moving scene in front of them. 'The plan is to turn all this area into parkland eventually; most of the old waterfront is gone already.'

'You disapprove?' she asked quietly as she began to eat, finding the hot, spicy food incredibly good.

'Unfortunately the bulldozer is not a discerning machine,' Melik said wryly. 'Admittedly the whole area was crumbling and less than enchanting but there are many facets in this ancient part of Istanbul worth saving and restoring. I think that maybe this is being recognised slowly. I hope the recognition has not come too late. With a city such as this one must tread carefully or improvements become a death-knell to the past.'

'You love this country, don't you?'

His dark face was alive with emotion. 'Of course, it is in my blood,' he answered proudly. 'Where else is there such a choice of beauty, such rich history? Nine thousand years of historical remains, troglodyte settlements and underground cities, relics from the dawn of civilisation at every corner.'

'You make it sound fascinating.' They seemed to be getting on safer ground and she relaxed a little more, eating a juicy cube of swordfish with its taste of the ocean and far-away places as the strong sea breeze fanned her hair into a golden cloud across her shoulders.

'I shall do more than that, my little tigress,' he said softly, and she tensed immediately; this was the first time he had called her by the old name since the night in his car and the easy use of it was confirmation of her worst fears. He had been biding his time after all, like the big dark-natured cat he reminded her of, biding his time and waiting. . .'I shall not be content until I have shown you the rolling hills and sunflower fields of Thrace, the snow-capped peaks of the mighty Taurus mountains, the white sands and translucent waters of the Mediterranean with its shores of pine forests, orange groves and banana plantations — all that and much, much more. You will grow to love this land as I do, love it and never want to leave.'

'I will?' She tried to laugh to break the mood of intimacy that he had woven but the sound stuck in her throat. 'I hardly think the few months I've got left here will be enough time for all that.'

'You think I will let you leave?' He took one of her hands in his, turning the palm over slowly and stroking the tiny pulse at the base of her wrist with persuasive fingers before raising her hand to his lips and kissing the soft interior of her palm with a slowly lingering caress. His mouth burnt, a hundred sensations leaping shockingly along her nerve-endings and causing her to wrench her hand from his grasp, her cheeks hot and her eyes bright.

'Don't.' She eyed him angrily. This was all part of the usual seduction scene, was it? The deep, rich, throaty voice and glittering flecked eyes that promised so much?

'Why not?' He eyed her flushed face and shaking hands with hard, speculative eyes. 'Is it because you want it too much?'

'No, I don't, of course I don't,' she protested immediately. 'I'm not into cheap affairs, Melik, so look for someone else to have a little diversion with if that's what you want.'

'A cheap affair?' For a moment she thought he was going to hit her as his face turned as black as thunder and his eyes blazed an icy light that stopped her heart from beating. 'Is that how you view a relationship between a man and a woman? As something cheap, something. . .unclean?' His gaze flashed over the English newspaper lying on the bench beside her and as he raised his eyes back to her face she saw a hard, biting contempt darken them still further. 'You are happy to live your life by watching the experiences of others? Of reading about life and love through the pages of your newspaper? Is that it?'

'That's unfair!' Anger was pumping welcome adrenalin into her system now to combat the trembling his rage had produced. 'Just because I don't fall gratefully into your arms the minute you beckon like all your other women, you needn't try and twist things.'

'All my other women?' He shut his eyes for a brief moment, his countenance black. 'I have many other women, is that it? I do not believe I am allowing this conversation to continue! And where do I keep all these other women, Louisa? Pray let the fairy-tale carry on; I am quite fascinated.'

'I don't suppose you exactly keep them anywhere,' she said icily, furious at the sarcasm. 'But you can't tell me they aren't around anyway; I'm not stupid, Melik.'

'That is a statement open to debate,' he ground out through gritted teeth. 'And where have you been hearing these so delightful stories about the big bad wolf and all the Little Red Riding Hoods? No, do not tell me, let me guess. The office staff?' He nodded slowly as she kept her head still and stiff in front of him. 'I might have guessed; that is it, isn't it? And you dare to say you are not stupid?'

'You aren't seriously trying to tell me you live the life of a monk?' she said furiously as the last thread of her self-control was broken by the insult.

'Oh, so now you are asking *me* to tell *you* something?' he spat furiously. 'How kind, how reasonable of you. What is it that you want to hear? Grovelling assurances that I am as pure as the driven snow? Protestations that I have never had a woman in my bed? Well, as you so rightly guessed, I cannot oblige with such untruths. Of course I have had women, Louisa; I am a thirty-seven-year-old man with a healthy body and appetites to match.'

If he had suddenly reached out and punched her in the stomach it would have been preferable to the pain that coursed through her body at the softly snarled words. But she had known, hadn't she? She caught at her shattered nerves desperately. She had known! What was so bad about hearing him put it into words?

'However, the difference between two people who find each other attractive enjoying a satisfying relationship for a time and the sort of picture you have painted

is enormous,' he continued icily. 'I have never pretended in the past that my feelings were those of
undying love as written about by the poets and such-
like. I have always been totally honest.'

'And they were content with that?' she asked
incredulously. 'They didn't want more?'

'Of course they were content with the situation,' he
said tightly, 'or I would not have done them the
injustice of getting involved in the first place. Not every
woman wants slippers by the fire or even a permanent
hearth in which to have a fire! And for the record there
have not been droves beating a path to my door. I
abhor promiscuity whether it be in the male or female
of the species.'

'I find that hard to believe.' She was totally out of
her depth and floundering badly, but there was no way
she was going to let him know that, she thought
painfully, forcing a scornful note into her voice to block
the trembling she was frightened he would hear.

'Doubtless.' It was clear from his taut body that her
attitude was not going a long way to diffuse the
situation. 'But as I do not have to justify myself to you
or anyone else it really doesn't matter, does it?' He
was being deliberately cruel and she steeled herself for
more of the same but he rose swiftly, pulling her up
and placing their half-full plates of now cold food on
the bench. 'Why the ivory tower, Louisa?'

A young Turkish family out for the evening, the
children dark and pretty and beautifully dressed,
passed them, smiling and nodding, as Melik inclined
his head.

'I said, why the ivory tower?'

'I heard you.'

'And you do not intend to reply,' he stated flatly,

slipping his arm through hers as they began to climb the steep cobbled path away from the noise and colour of the busy waterfront, the silvery moonlight filtering down between ancient houses on either side of the narrow, silent street. 'Well, you will tell me one day, Louisa, that I promise you. In fact, you will tell me all I want to know when the last defence is broken down and——'

'And I become just like any other woman?' she interrupted bitterly, incensed at his autocratic manner and the way he made her feel even when he was being at his most arrogant, like now.

It was this alien country, she told herself desperately, the seductive aura of the East that pervaded every nook and cranny and worked its lethally sensual magic in a land where for centuries it had been the normal way of life for one man to expect total and complete submission from the women he took for his own, a primal possessiveness in his bearing that had been accepted and considered natural.

The major face-lift of the last sixty years had changed some things, she thought helplessly, but still the insidiously voluptuous beauty of this diverse land had an ageless magic that lingered to beckon and entice and enthral. She had never burned to feel a man's hands on her body, his mouth pressed to hers before, never——

'Just like any other woman?' he said coldly, his tight voice jerking her eyes back to his face. 'I think you insult your sisterhood with such. . .sexist talk. No man or woman is like another in the way you suggest; we are all different. I am surprised you do not think this.'

'Of course I think it,' she shot back hotly, aware that he had done it again, turned things around until she was on the defensive and having to explain herself. 'I happen to believe men and woman are equal, that neither one should expect to dominate the other.'

'I agree.' She stared at him wide-eyed. He agreed? Never! 'Apart from just one place, that is. In the bedroom.'

'The bedroom?' she said slowly, hating the weakness in her voice.

'You have not found this so?' His face was in shadow, the tawny eyes veiled and closed against her, but she still felt as though the golden gaze was boring into her brain, seeking out that hidden part of her that even Oliver had not known existed.

'I don't want to discuss this any further.' She jerked herself from his grasp as the blood pounded through her ears. 'I think it would be better if I arranged for someone else to work with you. Most of the ground work is done now; someone else could easily —— '

He swore, softly and fluently in his own tongue, his eyes blazing now as they raked her face. 'Did I get too close for a moment?' His voice was icy in stark contrast to his face. 'What is his name, Louisa, the name of the man who has left you so empty and frightened of life? What the hell did he do to you anyway?'

'Just leave me alone!' She glared at him even as the shaking that had taken hold of her limbs transferred itself to her voice. 'I work for you, that's all; what do you think gives you the right —— ?'

'*Gives* me the right?' His voice was contemptuous and cold. 'You think I wait for life to *give* me the right? We're here once and once only, Louisa; you have to reach out and take what you want. . .' As he pulled her into his arms she began to struggle, her breathing quick and ragged, but it was as ineffectual as beating her fists against rock, his body immovable. She made to turn her head away but he was too quick, taking her lips in a hot, fierce kiss that explored her mouth with savage concentration.

She tried to fight him but even as her struggles ceased she knew it had been her own weakness she was frightened of, and so she should have been, she thought, panic-stricken, because it was happening again, that sweet, melting warmness that caused desire to flicker and then burn in a thudding flood.

His mouth was gentler now, even leisurely, his hands moving up underneath her coat to mould her shoulders further into him as he tasted her sweetness slowly, savouring each movement of his flickering tongue. He was drawing little shocks of sensation from every part of her body and he knew it; he knew the effect he had on her. Even as she felt the trembling that was shaking her limbs communicate itself to him she melted still further into his hard shape, accepting his mastery, his instinctive knowledge of how to conquer all her inhibitions, utterly vanquished beneath his expertise.

'And you would deny us this, my sweet, savage tigress?' he whispered huskily, his hands roaming over her body under the light coat and igniting shivers of fire wherever they touched. Her hands moved flutteringly up into his hair, almost of their own volition, and as he felt her fingers at the back of his neck he groaned softly and deeply against her mouth, the movement of his body against hers as he pressed her back against the wall in the shadowed darkness shockingly indicative of his arousal.

She had to stop this, had to. . . Her brain knew it but her body was helplessly caught in a drugged dreamlike state that was all the more thrilling because of its newness, the unknown shivers of passion and desire rendering her defenceless and abandoned in his arms. 'You are so beautiful, so sweet. . .' The whisper was faint against her ear and she responded blindly, a tangible ache that she had no will to resist engulfing her in its powerful need. 'You *will* be mine. . .'

The four small words brought her out of the fantasy he had woven with appalling suddenness and as she pushed against his chest his arms tightened briefly and then relaxed. 'What is it?' He moved back a pace as he spoke and she heard his breathing was harsh and unsteady although his face was hidden from her in the shadows. 'Don't be frightened; I would not harm a hair of your head.' Even through her distress she recognised the enormous self-control that was the master of his desire as well as her own, and although she was grateful that he had immediately responded to her withdrawal a tiny perverse part of her was angry that he could dismiss her so easily.

'Please take me back to the apartment.' She had to force the words through dry, shaking lips, her distress obvious, but he didn't try to dissuade her, simply taking her hand and beginning to walk up the dark street without saying a word for long moments as he fought to control his breathing.

'I will not allow you to bury yourself alive, do you understand this, Louisa?' His voice was low and deep but with a curious lack of expression that made his words all the more chilling. 'I do not know what has transpired in your life to make you the woman you now are, but I will know, one day.' He turned her round at the top of the alley as they came into the bright, noisy thoroughfare and she saw his eyes were slits of light, piercingly intent. 'Believe me, Louisa, I *will* know.'

CHAPTER FIVE

THE sharp knock at the apartment door early the next morning, as Louisa and Sandra were having breakfast still in their nighties, brought an immediate frown to Sandra's smooth brow. 'Oh, for goodness' sake, that woman gets earlier and earlier,' she hissed tightly at Louisa as she rose from the table with an angry flourish. 'I'm fed up with sharing a dolmuş with the old bat anyway; I'm going to tell her to go on if she's so desperate to get to the office and we'll follow when we're ready.'

'Sandra. . .' Louisa's voice rose warningly in the air just as Sandra reached the front door, but she grimaced defiantly before whisking open the front door with a swift display of irritation that died an immediate death before Melik's cool stare.

'Good morning.' He was the first one to find his voice, but then he would be, wouldn't he? Louisa thought nastily as she hastily reached for her robe on the back of the chair and pulled it over her thin cotton nightie with more haste than aplomb. *He* wasn't half naked. And what did he want?

'Oh, I'm sorry.' The sheer satin of Sandra's nightie left nothing to the imagination and she backed away from Melik as though he were the devil himself, her cheeky poise quite deserting her for once. 'I thought you were Mrs Jones, Mr Haman, but of course you're not. . .'

'No, I am not,' he agreed gravely, the sombre face

unable to hide the wicked dart of delighted amusement that burnt briefly in the glittering eyes.

'No. . .' Sandra backed right to the door of her bedroom and with a muttered, 'Excuse me,' disappeared into its sanctuary like a startled rabbit.

'I'd have called more often if I'd known,' he said drily. 'Am I allowed in?'

'Of course.' Louisa forced herself to move from behind the comforting bulk of the table even though the thigh-length robe revealed far more of her flesh than she would have liked. 'Would you like a coffee?' Play it cool, Louisa, cool. . .

'I'd love one.'

She was painfully aware of his eyes on her hair, which always curled in riotous, unrestrained curls around her face and shoulders after her morning shower before she trained it back into the severe style she wore for the office, but he said nothing, walking across the room in slow, measured steps and sitting down on the seat Sandra had vacated, his dark, brooding presence suddenly filling the whole flat.

'What can I do for you?' She turned with the coffee-mug as she spoke in time to see him shut his eyes for a brief moment, their flecked gaze brilliant when they opened a second later.

'I'm trying very hard to be professional this morning, Louisa,' he said flatly, 'but at the moment I'm losing ground fast. Before I show you exactly what you can do for me perhaps you ought to go and change into something. . .less comfortable? I'll sip my coffee like a good boy while I wait.'

She opened her mouth to speak and then shut it again quickly. He was absolutely right: she had been about to suggest the same thing herself.

When she re-emerged ten minutes later in a linen skirt and neat blue blouse, her hair sedately brushed into tight order, not a wisp escaping from the severe knot, both her mind and her body were under control again. She was English, practical, cool and down-to-earth, more suited to a walk in the rain in sensible brogues than a flight into fantasy in this hot, beautiful, wild land with its ancient customs and dark, untamed men, and she had better remember it. Last night had been a mistake, a grave mistake. She would not let him repeat it.

'There are a few problems that have arisen on my estate on the Black Sea coast.' He spoke immediately she entered the room, his voice cool and contained. 'I feel we have reached a plateau as far as the work here is concerned and can safely leave for a few days without a major catastrophe rearing its head. You agree?'

'Yes.' She looked at him warily. Why had that 'we' been slipped in there? He didn't seriously think ——

'My plane is waiting and I would like to leave this morning. Can you pack a case and be ready in half an hour?'

'Me?' She stared at him in horror. 'You don't expect me to come, surely?'

'Of course.' His voice was as cold as ice now and his face quite expressionless.

'But why?' She became aware that her voice was too shrill and lowered it hurriedly. Sandra was still in her room no doubt with her ear pressed to the keyhole! 'I can carry on with things here and——'

'I thought I had made the position perfectly clear when you first accepted the job?' he said tightly.

'But that proviso was if it was necessary——'

'I will decide what is necessary and what is not,' he

said coldly. 'Be ready in half an hour. My car will return for you then. Mrs Jones is fully acquainted with the details and you will be communicating with her every day by telephone. Do you understand?'

'No, I do not!' She would have liked to scream at him to dent the iron-hard composure but contented herself with a splinter-sharp reply. 'If I am reading you correctly you expect me to pack a bag and accompany you to goodness knows where at the drop of a hat. Is that about it?'

'Consider yourself a first-class reader, Louisa,' he said coolly. 'At the beginning of this assignment the facts were made very clear to you; please do not tax my patience or my time now by choosing to be difficult.'

She was still staring at him open-mouthed, amazed at the sheer audacity of the man, when he left, his handsome face expressionless and the big body confident and relaxed.

'What was all that about?' Sandra emerged at once from the bedroom in a cloud of perfume and goggle-eyed curiosity, turning on the flat's small radio as she did so, which immediately filled the small room with the wailing tones of Turkish music, the whining tune reminiscent of an Eastern chant.

'Sandra! Do you have to?' Louisa felt immediately ashamed of her snappishness but her friend just smiled knowingly, shaking her head as she cut off the unmelodious sound.

'He's getting to you, I knew he would. I could see it coming.'

'Don't be ridiculous.' Louisa drew herself up stiffly and prepared to march into her bedroom. 'He's got some business to attend to somewhere else and I've got to go with him. I'm going to pack.'

'Business?' Sandra's throaty chuckle was meant to annoy and annoy it did. 'That's not the first time I've heard it called that either. I've seen the way he looks at you!'

She was ready and waiting when Melik's chauffeur arrived thirty minutes later, waiting and gently simmering like hot, angry jam on the top of a stove.

'There has been a slight change of plan,' the stony-faced man told her impassively as he carried her case down to the waiting Mercedes. 'You will be meeting Mr Haman at the Galata Bridge.'

'Will I?' She hadn't known where she was going to meet him anyway so the news didn't mean anything to her.

As the Mercedes plunged into the four-lane highway, congested as always with a mixture of cars, buses, disreputable trucks and the odd horse-driven cart, she sank back into the luxurious seat and wondered if it was just her who was mad or the rest of the world. Mrs Jones had been as po-faced as normal when she had arrived to collect Sandra for the office, her whole attitude proclaiming that Louisa should count herself very lucky even to be considered for such a prestigious post, and her heavy eyebrows raising up into the steel-grey hair when Louisa had expressed her nervousness.

'Mr Haman is an extremely wealthy and well known businessman, Miss Collins,' she had said with scornful hauteur, her face rigid. 'He has offices in different countries all over the world; this Turkish project is just a drop in the ocean to him. Do you seriously think we can, for one moment, refuse to co-operate with him in any way?'

Sandra hadn't helped either when she had left, taking Louisa aside for a brief moment as she whispered in her ear, 'Co-operate with him? I'd eat him alive!' Her wink over Mrs Jones's shoulder as she had left had been lewd and lascivious, adding to the pounding of Louisa's heart. She should have refused to go, *she should have*!

They arrived at Galata Bridge, on the Karakoy side, at half-past nine, and she saw Melik immediately, her heart leaping into her mouth at the sight of his tall, broad figure as he scanned the moving traffic impatiently. As his eyes met hers through the window of the car she thought, for just a brief moment, that she saw an expression of profound relief on the hard features, but then as the car stopped and he helped her to alight she saw that his eyes were cool and distant, his mouth straight.

'Thank you for being prompt,' he said tightly, nodding to his chauffeur as he disappeared back into the traffic.

'Oh, my case is in there,' she said urgently, forgetting her antagonism for a moment at the prospect of losing all her clothes in one fell swoop.

'Calm yourself, Louisa. Osman will be meeting us soon,' he said shortly, 'but in the meantime I thought you might like to combine business with pleasure for once.' The twist to his mouth told her that he had not forgotten her earlier comment on the subject. 'We are travelling to my home on the Black Sea coast and a trip down the Bosporus takes us in the right direction. I thought at least you might appreciate the improving of your mind?'

Why did he have to make even the simplest comment loaded with hidden meaning that she was powerless to respond to? she asked herself irritably, although the excursion he was suggesting was one that she had promised herself ever since arriving in Istanbul. The nineteen-mile Bosporus, the winding strait separating Europe and Asia, had enough of the past and present scattered along its shores to satisfy even the most discerning traveller. Grand hotels, ancient wooden houses known as *yali*, splendid marble palaces and tiny picturesque fishing villages — they were all there in vibrant, colourful, roaming beauty which made the Bosporus the most scenic waterway of the world.

'Well?' Her eyes had been drawn to the seven hills dominating the skyline; the domed roofs of the Topkapi Palace, the regal silhouette of St Sophia, the breathtakingly majestic Süleymaniye Mosque, the Tower of Beyazit all visible and heart-stoppingly beautiful, and now as his voice called her back to him she turned wide eyes to meet his cool gold gaze. 'Are you prepared to endure my company for a few hours?' There was something in his voice, a throb of emotion, that she couldn't quite place but that somehow melted her resistance as effectively as a flame on ice.

'It's very kind of you to think of this, Melik,' she said softly, suddenly shy. 'Thank you.'

He stared at her for a long moment, his gaze piercing on her face, before smiling slowly and taking her arm as he pointed to a long, sleek, white-painted boat that was already half-full. 'Your transport awaits.'

She was glad the morning was so clear and bright as they set off a little while later; November fog had been evident in the last week and it would have spoilt the fantastic view up the Golden Horn where the hillsides were packed with ancient and modern buildings, pencil-slim minarets and towers galore.

'Comfortable?' As she dragged her eyes away from the Dolmabahçe Palace spread comfortably along the shore, the shafts of sunlight from the clear blue sky overhead turning it into picture-postcard handsomeness, she met Melik's warm gaze. He was sitting with his arm casually draped round her shoulders and although she had stiffened at first, her body instinctively freezing at the physical contact, the unfurling scene in front of her had soon claimed total absorption.

'It's so beautiful.' Palaces, majestic gardens, splendid hotels and luxurious waterside villas had given way to tiny villages, the delightful, two-storey wooden houses with carved beams wonderfully picturesque.

For the rest of her life she was to remember that trip down the Bosporus, with Melik warm and companionable at her side while he explained the different sights that crowded in on her entranced gaze before she could draw breath, as a time unreal and breathtakingly magical. The past and present, intrinsically linked by the mixture of ancient and modern, was suddenly enough for the moment; there was no future, no tomorrows, no rejection, no goodbyes. . .

'You see there?' Melik leant over her slightly to point ahead and as the faint scent of him surrounded her in its intoxicatingly sensual attraction her heart pounded violently. His hard thigh was pressed against her softness, his arm was tight against her shoulders now as he held her against him, and she was vitally conscious of the leashed power of the big body, the hard masculine limbs and strong, broad chest. Would he ever marry? The thought popped unbidden into her mind and once there flourished. Did men like him ever *really* marry or did they just join their name to a suitable partner for business or social reasons, a family, the linking of estates? She forced the train of thought to stop abruptly and concentrated on what he was saying, his clean breath warm against her cheek.

'You see at the narrowest point the two castles?' he was asking softly. 'They played a key role in the Turkish conquest of Constantinople.'

'They did?' She found the nearness of his hard square jaw, faintly dusky with the swift growth of his beard, far more fascinating than the two mighty castles in spite of their history.

'The first castle on the Asian side was built in 1395,' Melik continued, 'to enforfce the control of maritime traffic to and from the Black Sea. Then Mehmet the Conqueror, at the young age of twenty-one, had the Rumeli Hisari fortress built on the European side so total domination was accomplished by the Turkish forces. The whole thing from start to finish took just nineteen weeks to complete, with an army of workers and a thousand skilled masons working day and night. Turks, even at that tender age, can be quite ruthless when they want something,' he added expressionlessly. 'It is not natural for the word "failure" to feature in our vocabulary.'

As the golden gaze turned down to her she saw there was a heat in the beautiful eyes, a banked-down glow, that caused the blood to pound through her veins. 'And no?' she asked softly. 'Does the word "no" have any effect on the Turks?'

He smiled slowly, his handsome face magnificently male. 'Only if we allow it.'

'I think I've figured that out for myself,' she said after a long still moment, her back straight now.

'Have you?' His gaze lingered on her mouth for a second before turning to the castles. 'I don't think so, not yet, but you will. The inner courtyard in the Rumeli castle is used for open-air theatre now,' he continued blandly as though all they had been discussing were architecture and history, 'and they have concerts and folklore shows there too. Have you been to a folklore evening yet?'

She shook her head silently.

'The fierce Mrs Jones again?'

She didn't return his smile; it was taking all her will to calm her racing heart into submission. 'That and work,' she said shortly.

'Of course.' He shook his black head slowly. 'I have not left you with sufficient time for such pleasure, have I, working you day and night? I will make amends, I promise.'

'I don't want you to make amends,' she said urgently, aware that she had played straight into his hands, and what large, capable hands too! 'I've done the job I was paid to do, that's all.'

'I disagree.' It was the end of the conversation as far as he was concerned.

As they slowly travelled past beautiful little water-side villages, sleepy and quiet in the mild November sun, the odd elderly Turk sitting meditatively with his hubble-bubble pipe amid green fishing boats and colourful little blue and yellow houses, the tranquillity of it all was overpoweringly poignant. Soon it would end, Louisa thought helplessly, and she would be plunged back into the turmoil and confusion that seemed to have been with her ever since she had first laid eyes on this big, dangerous man. And she could do nothing about it. Nothing at all. The thought was not comforting.

When they docked it was to find the chauffeur

waiting impassively at the end of the quay, the powerful car parked broodingly in the afternoon sun. 'The end of the Bosporus is a closed military zone,' Melik informed her quietly as he seated her in the Mercedes's comfortable seat, 'and as we do not wish to tangle with the authorities we will now resume our journey by car, yes?'

'It was a lovely trip, Melik.' She touched his arm hesitantly as he sat with his face in profile to her, looking out of the window. 'Thank you.'

'My pleasure.' He turned, his eyes soft. 'If a trip down the Bosporus is all it takes to hear you say my name so prettily then we will do it every day. You rarely do, you know. . .say my name.'

'Do I?' She blushed hotly, knowing full well she found it difficult. It seemed too intimate somehow, too friendly, especially when everyone else in the office apart from Mr Ashton addressed him formally. And he wasn't a man it was easy to be informal with. Apart from the knowledge that he was immensely wealthy and dangerously powerful the very maleness of him, the overwhelming physical attraction she felt for him, kept her tongue tied very often in a way it had never been before. And she did find him so physically devastating. The thought was something of a shock and she realised she had never faced it before.

'You know damn well you do,' he said shortly. 'And that's another thing that's going to change in the next few days. You can hardly stay in my house, eating my food, sleeping in. . .one of my beds without using my Christian name, can you?' He smiled wickedly at her red cheeks. 'Can you?'

'Of course not,' she snapped quickly. He was infuriating, absolutely and utterly infuriating; he never missed an opportunity to get under her skin! 'But I do understand I'm still working so don't worry I'll take advantage.'

He eyed her long and seriously until at last, much to her chagrin, she was forced to look away from the piercingly intent tawny eyes. 'I am sure there is Turkish blood flowing somewhere in that delectable body,' he said at last with a deep sigh as he folded his arms across his chest and settled further down in the seat, shutting his eyes and allowing his big body to relax. 'You sure don't give up, do you?'

She didn't, couldn't reply, and they travelled for a few miles in silence before he spoke again. 'We will be stopping shortly for a late lunch. I normally travel home from Istanbul by air as the roads are not conducive to fast motoring, although the coastal road we are on now is adequate. However, I thought you might like to see a little of the countryside.'

'Thank you.' There was nothing else she could say.

They stopped for lunch a short time later at a caravanserai, an old stone inn where once ancient traders rested and ate a meal free of charge, which had been converted to a modern-day motel.

The meal was excellent and Louisa found that the trip down the Bosporus in the fresh, salty air had given her a ravenous appetite. They feasted on *lahmacun*, Turkish pizza, although the delicious concoction tasted like no pizza Louisa had tried before. A thin, crisp dough had been topped with ground lamb, onions, cheese and spices and when served with ice-cold, frothy *ayra*, a fortifying drink of beaten yoghurt, spring water and a dash of salt, the *lahmacun*, served hot and steaming out of the wood-burning oven, was mouthwateringly good.

'That was out of this world,' Louisa murmured with replete satisfaction as she finished her last mouthful, leaning back in her seat with a little sigh of contentment. 'Absolutely out of this world.' She raised her eyes to find Melik's amused gaze warm on her face. 'Well, it was,' she repeated a little indignantly as he eyed her smilingly.

'I agree.' He let his gaze wander over her body in a frank approval that brought the blood surging into her cheeks. 'I was just wondering how one so tiny could fit so much food into such a slender shape.'

'I think if I stayed too long in your country I wouldn't have a slender shape,' she countered quickly.

'That would not matter.' Now the amusement had left his face and his eyes were deadly serious as they held hers with their golden light. 'Slim, plump, old, young, you would still be beautiful, little tigress.'

'I doubt it.' She tried to laugh, to break the intimate mood; the look in his eyes was unnerving. 'You men are very good at saying things like that!'

'You think I am merely saying what you would like to hear? That I am flattering you?'

She stared at him warily. That was exactly what she thought but from the look on his face he wouldn't like hearing her say so, and she had to spend at least a few days locked away with him in this home of his wherever it was. 'I think you are being pleasant,' she hedged carefully, 'that's all.'

'Oh, Louisa. . .' He shook his head slowly, his eyes narrowed and gleaming in the tanned darkness of his face. 'How am I ever going to get through to you, my cautious English rose? You are twenty-eight years of age and yet there are times when I could almost think that you are as innocent and untouched as a virginal fifteen-year-old, if it were not impossible with that hair and those eyes. When are you going to come out of your shell and start living again, tasting life and love again? Whatever happened, whether it be a man or something else, it is not worth such a sacrificial offering of a life. Don't you see?'

'Melik, I don't want to discuss——'

'I'm not interested in what you *do not* want,' he said softly, his eyes glittering. 'I have held you in my arms, I have felt your heart beating under mine; you cannot hide what you feel, Louisa.'

'You are saying you feel I am physically attracted to you?' she said flatly, summoning all her strength to project an image of cool distaste when her heart was pounding so violently it was making her feel sick. 'Well, so what if I am? I'm sure it's not a first with you and there must be lots of women only too happy to oblige mutual lust by jumping immediately into bed at the first sign of sexual compatibility. Unfortunately I am not one of them. I've met a lot of men I've found attractive,' she lied expressionlessly, 'but it doesn't mean I've gone to bed with all of them.'

He stared at her for a full minute, his face curiously enigmatic. She had expected offended pride, rage, hot and cutting words, but when he spoke his voice was reflective, thoughtful even. 'You are being offensive and uncharacteristically cruel. Now why?' He leant across the tiny wooden table and took her chin in his hand, forcing her eyes up to meet his as he looked long and hard in their deep brown depths. 'This intrigues me. You intrigue me.'

'Do I indeed!' She jerked away sharply, her skin tingling at his touch and her nerves jumping. 'Well, I'm sorry but I can't return the compliment.'

'Now you are being childish,' he remarked crushingly. 'My culture rates good manners highly, not just in a social sense but as a means of expressing care and affection for whoever it may be, stranger or friend. I have noticed that your gentleness is an intrinsic part of your nature, it has not had to be learnt, and you are fighting this now with me. Does what you feel frighten you so much?'

He was intuitive, she had to give him that, she thought angrily, but just at this moment in time she would have given all she possessed to wipe the superior awareness from that good-looking face. His eyes were warm and perceptive as they searched hers but she didn't trust that expression of concern, the all-too-obvious examining of her emotions. A man like him wanted a woman like her, a virtual nobody in his world, for one reason and one reason only. Dress it up how you like, she thought bitterly, but it was the law of the jungle. Like the big cat he reminded her of he would not be satisfied with one woman for long and as the lion gathered his lionesses around him in harem-like submission, so he would expect the freedom to wander where he would.

'Doesn't the thought that you might be wrong about things ever come into your mind?' she asked as coolly as her burning cheeks would allow. 'You may have grown up thinking you were the mighty and all-powerful one, no doubt aided and abetted by your parents, but frankly I find such an attitude distasteful in the extreme. You think you will always get what you want just because you want it, don't you? *Don't* you?'

'Yes.' His eyes had hardened and narrowed as her voice had progressed but his voice was quite without apology, clipped and sharp. 'That is exactly what I think.'

'Well, not in this case,' she said cuttingly. 'I'm a person, Melik, not a walking doll on two legs, and I place a higher value on myself than obviously you do.'

She had hit him on the raw at last. She saw it in the way his eyes suddenly blazed a cold fire that made her skin prickle and the hairs on the back of her neck rise in protest. He was angry, furiously, smoulderingly angry, and she was immensely glad of the other diners as he glared at her, his eyes flashing.

'You deserve to be whipped for that,' he snarled savagely. 'Whipped to within an inch of your life.'

'Oh, so now we're back to the old days all of a sudden, are we?' she countered bitingly although inside her stomach had turned to melted jelly and her legs felt as though they had just been run over by a steamroller. 'As soon as you meet with a little resistance, a woman who doesn't see things your way, it's back to the sultan approach with force and whips? Charming, absolutely charming.'

The oath that spat from his lips made her very glad her knowledge of Turkish was so limited, and then she was up and out of her seat as he grasped her arm and virtually dragged her out to the car, throwing her into the back seat with a glowering nod at the driver who seemed to shrink down in his seat a good few inches as they started off.

'You are the most impossible woman I have ever had the misfortune to meet,' he said tightly after several electric minutes had ticked by, the atmosphere so hot that she wouldn't have been surprised if the expensive upholstery had begun to melt. 'Argumentative, difficult, exasperating and ridiculously independent.'

She didn't reply; there was nothing on reflection she could add to what he had already said, and in spite of his tone and the set, cold face as he stared straight ahead at the chauffeur's dark head through the tinted-glass panel she didn't altogether disagree with his summing-up. There were other aspects to her personality he could have mentioned but if she was honest he had only seen what she had been prepared to let him see so far, and in the main she felt the words he had used were quite mild. She didn't have much to arm herself with as far as this man was concerned; she was painfully aware that he seemed to touch a spot in her that was quite raw and unprotected, and she had to make use of every weapon to hand.

He could destroy her so easily. She risked a careful glance under her lashes and found he had shut his eyes, his face still like stone. He made her feel vulnerable, frightened, helpless, excited, so many things that she couldn't even acknowledge what half of them were, but underlying them all was a deep and powerful emotion that she didn't recognise and couldn't understand—but it scared her to death.

The resentment, hurt and pain she had always felt with her parents, the loneliness, the gnawing loneliness that had seemed ten times worse since Oliver had gone, the heartache and agonising desperation when he had died, all these were as nothing compared to how Melik could make her suffer if she were foolish enough to let him into her mind and body. She knew it. She didn't know how or why but she just knew it.

CHAPTER SIX

THE rest of the journey was painfully beautiful in marked contrast to Louisa's thoughts: lushly forested mountains plunging dangerously into crystal-clear unpolluted seas, ripe hazelnut groves, tea terraces, sprawling tobacco plantations green and rich in the afternoon sun, tiny sandy beaches as well as seashores of black pebbles from which the sea got its name, all fitted between craggy projections of rock that were as mighty as they were dangerous. . . So much wild *and* tamed beauty and so unexpected. The noise and frantic bustle of Istanbul seemed another lifetime away.

She had read somewhere that according to legend the Black Sea shores were the land of the Amazons, that fierce tribe of female warriors who had competed with men and reigned supreme, and as they went on into the dusky evening she found herself reaching out to the long-dead Amazons, asking for some of their strength for the days that lay ahead.

It was almost dark when they reached their destination, the sky a soft indigo-blue velvet canopy under which Melik's tea plantation stretched endlessly along a vast mountain slope.

'Tea?' She had stared at him in amazement when he had explained what the estate entailed. 'I didn't know you were into tea.'

'I am probably "into" many activities of which you know nothing,' he had returned drily, his cool face betraying the fact that he had not quite forgiven her for her earlier defiance. 'However, this is the ancestral home of the Hamans, as it happens; I was born here.'

'Were you?' She stared at the handsome closed face in fascination as the big car purred through massive gates after climbing steadily for twenty minutes or more.

He nodded slowly as they scrunched along on a beautifully laid road in marked contrast to the rough lanes they had been travelling on a few miles before. 'My mother was booked into the finest hospital in Turkey, so I understand — my father was desperate nothing should go wrong — but they were here seeing to some estate problems when she was eight months pregnant and I decided I had waited long enough to see the world, and was born within an hour of announcing my arrival was imminent. She was still clutching a leaf of tea in her hand when it was all over, or so she says,' he finished quietly.

'Why tea? Why did your family decide to grow tea?'

'Why not?' He turned to fix her with his tawny gaze, his expression indicating slight surprise at her curiosity. 'The main export crops are cotton, tobacco, fruit and nuts but my grandfather changed to tea for reasons of his own and now, since 1945, Turkey grows all its own tea in this area; we're self-sufficient.' He smiled slowly. 'I've no complaints; we did well out of it all. The men in my family all seemed to marry well, bringing more wealth into the Haman fortunes, and now the business interests are vast — vast and time-consuming,' he added ruefully. 'This estate is a relaxing hobby in comparison.'

'Oh.' She smiled flatly. His words only confirmed her earlier thoughts. He would marry for convenience and marry well. It would be expected. The small dart of pain that cut off her breath for a second was unexpected and unwelcome.

Either side of the road alder, lime and elm trees grew wide and tall, a mass of rhododendrons, arbutus and yellow azalea in bloom in the sheltered regions underneath, and then as they turned a sharp corner the house was there in front of her and within a second they were in front of the huge pillars guarding the arched doorway.

She realised, as she gazed at the magnificent huge old house, that she had been mentally preparing herself for something like this for the last fifty miles or so, but nevertheless it still took her breath away.

The house had been painted in traditional white, with massive full-length windows on the second and third floors opening on to intricately wrought iron balconies from which a profusion of vividly coloured winding flowers hung down in gay contrast to the white-painted walls. The sloping roof was red-tiled, the mass of red and green ivy that clung in gay abandon to the walls reaching almost to its stately contours, and the whole effect was one of stunning colour, graciousness and cool, tranquil peace.

'I don't know how you can ever bear to leave this place,' she said softly as she stared transfixed out of the car window, unaware of Melik's eyes warm and satisfied on her face as he took in her rapt appreciation of his home.

By the time he had walked round the car to open her door his face was set in the hard, chiselled lines she knew so well, calm, controlled and giving nothing away. 'It is beautiful, isn't it?' he agreed quietly as he took her arm and led her across the wide pebbled drive towards the front door. 'I am a most fortunate man.'

A single star had just made its appearance in the soft dusky sky, the air was perfumed with a thousand heavy scents from which she could just pick out honeysuckle and jasmine and as the chauffeur drove the car round the side of the house, disappearing from view, Melik suddenly stopped, his expression veiled and strange.

'Welcome to my home, Louisa.' He had taken her in his arms before she knew what he was doing and before she had time to resist, his mouth hot and sweet on hers as he took her mouth in a long, fierce kiss. And then she was free again, swaying slightly as she stared up into his dark face.

'Do you always welcome your employees like that?' she asked shakily as she took a step backwards.

'Not always.' His voice was dry. 'But maybe, if they all taste as good as you, I should start a precedent.'

'I don't think that would be a good idea.' She tried to match her voice and manner to his, to dismiss the kiss as unimportant although it was hard with the feel of his mouth still on hers and the smell of him in her nostrils. 'You're likely to have a host of angry husbands and boyfriends turning up on your doorstep.'

'But you do not have a husband Louisa, do you?' he stated silkily. 'Or a boyfriend either, for that matter. So, in your case. . .'

As he took a step towards her she stepped back again, her eyes flashing. 'Oh, no, once was a welcome, twice would be verging on the ingratiating, don't you think?'

'Not ingratiating, my little tigress.' Now there was a thread of steel in the velvet voice. 'I am a cruel and vicious sultan, remember; whips and chains are far more my style, as you so rightly pointed out, and now that you are in my domain I have you at my mercy. Isn't that the way you see it?'

'Hardly.' She eyed him with far more scorn than she was feeling inside. 'This is the twentieth century, remember.'

'Ah, yes, I had forgotten.' He smiled a smile reminiscent of a cat with a very large bowl of cream. 'In that case all I can do is to ask you to grace my humble home with your beauty and charm.'

'And sarcasm is the lowest form of wit,' she muttered darkly as the front doors were flung wide and a horde of servants, or so it seemed, appeared in the doorway.

'They are eager to meet you; come and be introduced,' Melik said quietly in her ear as he led her through the large arched doorway, picked out in tiny tiles in varying shades of blue and green in a fan-type pattern, and into the large, airy hall. She just had time to notice that a handsome Turkish carpet was covering most of the huge hall's shining wooden floor and take in a highly decorated and magnificent vase standing a full six feet in a quiet alcove, before Melik drew her further into his side as he introduced her to his staff, who bobbed a polite curtsy at their names.

'What are they doing that for?' she whispered to Melik, highly embarrassed. 'Don't they know I'm employed by you too?'

'It's different.' He eyed her unsmilingly. 'Trust me.'

The 'horde' shrunk into Safiye, the somewhat rotund housekeeper, her husband, Tegrul, who was Melik's estate manager and who inclined his head politely towards Louisa before disappearing through a side-door into the back of the house, and Cybiele and Kathi, the two maids who were small and dark and remarkably alike.

She mentioned this fact later to Melik at dinner, as they sat alone at the huge, beautifully engraved dining-table, a work of art in itself with gold and silver leaf worked beautifully into exquisite patterns of Eastern splendour. The whole house was the same, vast, beautiful and terrifyingly intimidating.

'Cybiele and Kathi?' He nodded slowly. 'They are twins, I understand, but not identical. Their family was killed in the political unrest of the 1970s and my father found them through a friend who ran an orphanage in the capital when they were just three months old. Safiye and Tegrul are unable to have children and so, after a mass of red tape, the babies were brought here in 1973 to the mutual satisfaction of all concerned.'

'Why did he do that?' she asked in amazement. 'I mean, Safiye and Tegrul are just employees——'

'You do not understand.' He leant forward, his eyes intense and his body powerful in the dim light from the beautiful old oil lamps scattered strategically round the glowing room. 'Tegrul's family has always served my family; they have been loyal and faithful and trust-worthy. They were my father's responsibility as they are now mine. It was right that he, as their protector, should do all in his power to bring them happiness. It is a matter of honour.'

'I see.' She was way out of her depth here, she thought helplessly. 'Do you consider all your employ-ees your responsibility, then?'

'Here on my estate, yes.' He settled back in his chair, the big bulk of him suiting the magnificent room and sumptuous furnishings, very much the master of his own empire.

He actually *looked* like a sultan, she thought sud-denly, especially in the open-necked, full-sleeved embroidered shirt he was wearing over loose white cotton trousers. The cool Western businessman had vanished as though he had been a figment of her imagination. Here he was all Turkish, dark, proud and very unapproachable, and terrifyingly attractive.

'The members of my household and those of the workers on the estate are under my protection and care,' he continued quietly, his eyes iridescent in the flickering light. 'It is my duty to watch over them, provide for their needs; it is a matter of trust. In return I expect total loyalty and unquestioning obedience.'

'You consider them your slaves?' she asked faintly as his tanned skin and black hair melted into the shadows until only the green-gold eyes seemed alive.

'My slaves?' He leant forward abruptly, bringing his face into startling vision, and she saw he was frowning, his black brows heavy over icy cold eyes. 'Are you trying to annoy me, Louisa?'

She was saved a reply by the arrival of Cybiele and Kathi with a huge loaded trolley containing a vast quantity of covered dishes which, after removing the soup dishes, they proceeded to place in the centre of the table before moving to stand quietly behind Melik's chair. 'Would you like to indicate which dishes you prefer?' he asked quietly.

'I. . .I don't know,' she answered vaguely as she glanced with something akin to horror at the massive choice.

He spoke in rapid Turkish to the two small girls and within seconds her plate was full of wonderfully aromatic food, half of which was totally new to her. It all proved delicious.

Dessert was nothing more adventurous than peeled fresh almonds mounded on a bed of ice and sliced apricots, peaches, cherries and grapes marinated in a light wine and served with a dash of brandy and thick fresh cream.

'Would you care for more wine?' Melik had been the perfect host, courteous although more than a little distant, and now as he refilled her enormous crystal wine glass with the light sparkling pink wine she raised her eyes to his enquiringly.

'It's lovely, what's it called?'

'Harem.' He eyed her wickedly, his face perfectly serious. 'I thought you would like it. I have it delivered especially from Thrace.'

'Oh.' She smiled weakly. 'Well, it's lovely. . .'

The sultry perfumes of musk and jasmine were heavy in the room from tiny solid blocks placed in lacy pottery jars on the marble fireplace that ran along half the length of one wall, the air was thick and warm and lazy, the deceptively light wine in the enormous glasses was making her head whirl a little, and suddenly Louisa felt she had to escape.

'Could I. . .could I have some air?' She half rose as she spoke. 'I feel a little faint, the long ride. . .'

'Of course.' He was at her side immediately, taking her arm as he gestured for the maids to clear the table as they reappeared right on cue. 'The courtyard is through here.' He indicated the open latticed doors at the end of the room. 'The gardens are beyond that but I would suggest you allow me to show you those tomorrow.'

Of course! It just had to be, didn't it? Louisa thought with an overwhelming sense of helplessness as she walked through the arched doorway into a beautifully intimate little courtyard surrounded by flowering almond trees rich with heavy, intoxicating blossom and tiny rustling fountains sparkling magically in the moon-light — an *Arabian Nights* scene of total sensuality guaranteed to melt even the most determined female heart. Was this his *fait accompli*? The place where he brought those women who were foolish enough to resist his advances, if there were any?

'Why so tense?' His shirt had fallen open to reveal the hair-roughened, muscled flesh she had just known was beneath, and Louisa found she was quite incapable of tearing her eyes away from his body. This may be planned, she thought desperately, and it may be a practised technique, but it was a prize formula.

'I have dreamed of seeing you here.' He hadn't touched her since they had walked through the doors but every nerve in her body was as sensitised as though they had been making love for hours. 'Clothed in silk, your hair flowing free. . .'

'Whereas I'm in sensible cotton.' She forced a bright smile to her lips as she gestured at the pretty sleeveless evening dress that she had bought as a safeguard for any situation, formal or informal.

'Half of my fantasy can be realised.' He removed the clip from her hair with practised ease before she could protest. 'And incidentally I forbid you to wear these things while you are here.' He flung the slides disdain-fully to the floor. 'They displease me.'

He even sounded different, she thought despairingly, his accent so pronounced that his words seemed to flow and ebb in a soft, silky tide that was seductively rich. 'Well, I'm *so* sorry,' she began sarcastically. 'If I'd only known——'

She was enclosed in his embrace before she could finish, his lips tasting her half-open mouth as his hands ran over her bare arms, his naked chest prickly against the soft swell of her breasts in the low-cut evening dress. The smell of him encompassed her, sensual, dark and altogether satisfying. 'You're mine, you *are* mine. . .' The kisses were tender and sweet and coaxing and with a mindless groan she knew she was lost. Force she could have resisted, violence she would have fought, but this. . . This was heavenly.

His mouth moved down to her throat, kissing the pulse beating so frantically, and then further downwards, brushing her silky skin with warm, teasing kisses that brought tiny little whimpers of delight from her half-open mouth. She wanted to resist, wanted to say no, but it was so unbearably sweet. . .

'I *can* make you forget.' His voice was low and fierce with triumph as he raised his head to look into the dazed blackness of her eyes. 'Whatever has happened, however bad it may be, I can make you forget. I will brand you, brand you as mine, until the past will be a dream that no longer belongs to you and the future will have only one name — mine!'

'Melik. . .'

'You have had no past, do you understand me? I will be the first, the only one, a new beginning. I will not *allow* it to be any other way.'

Maybe it was possible, she thought dazedly, as the last weeks and months in his powerful ruthless presence took their toll. If he wanted her, really wanted *her*, the complete person he had talked about once before, perhaps they had a chance? Knowing him as she did now, having seen his energy and the vehement force of his spirit, she knew he was strong enough to lay all the ghosts that hung round her, dismissing them with the authority that was natural to him. And maybe he wouldn't reject her the way her parents had, leave her like Oliver? Maybe. . .

'I will utterly possess you.' As his lovemaking reached new heights she felt she would faint with the pleasure he was inducing. 'Everything that you are will belong to me; I will be your world as you will be mine.'

His lips left a trail of fire as they burnt over the silky skin beneath his mouth and his hands were knowing as they played over the womanly curves beneath his fingertips. 'Talk to me, Louisa, tell me I am right — that I am speaking the desires of your heart.'

The tinkling of the tiny bell at one side of the curved archway that led from the house hardly registered on her whirling senses but he raised his head at the sound, his breathing harsh and ragged as he fought for control. 'There are guests. . .' He took a few long deep breaths as he looked down into her upturned face. 'Someone has opened the front door; we must have visitors.'

'Visitors?' She was trembling but she couldn't help it; but for his arms still supporting her she would have sunk to the floor.

'Here.' He adjusted her clothing with deft, quick fingers and then pushed her gently on to a smooth curved wooden seat at the side of an enormous tub of trailing, conical-shaped flowers whose heavy, sweet fragrance was reminiscent of roses and lilac. 'I will endeavour——'

What he would have endeavoured she would never know as at that moment Safiye appeared in the door-way after a discreet cough to announce her presence, speaking rapidly to Melik in Turkish, a few seconds before another voice, a young female voice, cut in behind her.

'*Melik*. . .' The voice was throaty and low and blatantly inviting. '*Nasilsiniz*?'

'I am fine, thank you, Lala,' Melik said smoothly. 'May I introduce Louisa? She knows only a little Turkish so if we could speak in English. . .?'

As Melik moved to one side she stood up hastily, and then wished with all her heart she had remained seated as the jolt in her stomach communicated itself to her legs. The young woman in front of her who had just slipped her hand through Melik's arm in one of those gestures that a man thought was perfectly innocent and another woman knew was a stamp of possession was quite strikingly beautiful. Tall, slim and voluptuous, she had smooth, silky brown skin exquisitely offset by heavy, shining jet-black hair that hung to her waist in sleek waves and exotic sloe eyes under beautifully shaped brows that were now raised in polite enquiry as they swept over Louisa's flushed face. Louisa felt her heart sink.

'Louisa?' Lala smiled just enough to show pearly white teeth between full, sensual lips. 'I do not think I have heard this name before?'

The request for an explanation was obvious but as Melik ignored it Louisa assumed she should. 'It's nice to meet you.' She smiled warmly. 'How do you do?'

'Louisa is staying with me for a few days,' Melik interposed smoothly as he took Louisa's arm in his and walked, still with Lala glued to his other side, under the archway and through the dining-room to the large living-room beyond. 'We are working on a project together.'

'You are?' As Lala sank down on to one of the low silk-upholstered divans that were scattered, Eastern fashion, around the carpeted floor she smiled up at

Louisa coldly. 'But how nice. You must tell me about it.'

'Lala and her parents are our nearest neighbours.' Melik walked over to the well stocked drinks cabinet on the far side of the room. 'We are old friends, are we not?'

'But of course.' The slanted eyes flashed over Melik hungrily and then turned back to Louisa, the soft brown becoming jet-hard. 'You are English, I understand? You are here for a short time only?' The full mouth was hostile and tight.

'We all have a twelve-month work permit,' Louisa said quietly, trying to curb the instinctive reaction of dislike she felt at the other girl's veiled aggressiveness. 'I leave around the middle of August next year.'

'Or not as the case may be.' Melik's voice was silky soft as he dropped his little stone into the already widening ripples. 'I know Lala will be drinking raki, a practice her parents heartily disapprove of. Louisa, you would like. . .?'

'Just a soft drink, please,' Louisa said quickly; the wine at dinner had been far too potent. 'Lemonade if you have it?' She wasn't fond of raki, a distillation of grape mash flavoured with aniseed, in spite of it being the national drink popularly known as 'lion's milk'. And Melik knew Lala's preferences, did he? She tried to control the trembling deep inside that was a combination of his lovemaking and the sudden arrival of this *femme fatale* who was clearly staking her claim.

'And Melik has brought you here for the wedding. How nice.' Whatever Lala thought about her arrival here, 'nice' in no way described it, Louisa thought painfully as she felt the full force of the ebony eyes a second before they switched to neutral. And what was this about a wedding? 'It's rather sweet, Melik, isn't it?' The beautiful face gave a practised smile that would melt the hardest male heart. 'One of your workers and one of ours meeting in the fields as they worked and love blooming among the tea terraces.'

'Quite.' Melik clearly wanted to change the subject but Lala turned to Louisa with another twist to her lips that now her face was turned away from the object of her devotion didn't even try to resemble a smile. 'And they were so charming about it all, waiting until the autumn when most of the crops have been harvested so that we could all really enjoy it. We're just one big family really, aren't we, Melik?'

And I'm the outsider—yes, I do get the picture, Louisa thought slowly, faintly amazed at the other girl's uncalled-for antagonism and her ability to project it while keeping Melik completely in the dark. Had she been involved romantically with him? Her heart thudded violently and then lurched on. *Was* she involved romantically with him? She certainly seemed to think she had some sort of proprietorial claim to him anyway. The sickening butterflies that had been fluttering madly in her stomach since the lovely Turkish girl had arrived suddenly went wild. Surely he wouldn't bring her, Louisa, here if that were the case, knowing they would be bound to meet? But then he might. She really knew nothing about him after all, and to think that a few minutes ago she had been considering. . .

'You must bring Louisa over to dinner while she is here,' Lala continued sweetly, earning a warm glance from Melik in the process which made Louisa's toes curl. 'I'm sure Mother and Father would love to meet her.'

'Thank you.' Louisa forced herself to smile as

Melik's eyes switched to her face. 'You live close by, then?'

'Close by for these parts; the estates do tend to sprawl somewhat.' Lala's voice was cultured and beautifully correct; she was obviously extremely well educated, Louisa thought miserably. 'Our respective families have been entwined for generations, haven't they, darling?' She flashed Melik a smouldering-hot smile. 'Melik grew up with my brothers; they were a dreadful pack of scoundrels.'

'Steady now, steady.' Melik laughed softly, his face more relaxed and easy than Louisa had ever seen it. 'Don't blacken my name on hearsay when I am trying to make a good impression on Louisa. You were too young to know anything about it anyway.'

Lala pouted prettily and Louisa's nostrils flared in distaste. What a coquette! But she was very good at it.

'Not that young! I am twenty-four now and perfectly grown-up but I still remember it was you who would allow me to tag along or ride with you on your horse.' Lala shifted slightly in her seat so that the tight, clinging sleeveless top she wore over baggy blue jeans moved in all the right places and the long gold hoops in her ears caught a flash of light that illuminated the golden skin. 'You've always been there for me, haven't you. . .?' She sent a long, lingering glance of complicity Melik's way.

'Well, you were a plucky little kid.' Melik smiled slowly. 'Plucky and very determined.'

She really couldn't take much more of this without being sick! Louisa moved abruptly in her seat and then gasped as ice-cold lemonade fizzed into her lap. Great! Just great.

'Oh, dear.' Lala's slanted eyes smiled in satisfaction.

'Now you will have to go and change, but do not worry, I will keep Melik occupied for you. We have loads to discuss about the wedding; Father has given me a list for you to look over,' she continued, turning to Melik as though Louisa had already left the room. 'He asked me to tell you that the priest is coming tomorrow.'

'Yes, I know.' Melik's voice was preoccupied and his gaze on Louisa as she arose, shaking her wet skirt slightly. 'I'll have another drink ready for when you return.'

'Don't bother.' He would never know the effort it cost her to force the bright, untroubled smile to her face as she gazed down at them both, Lala having moved to sit on the arm of Melik's chair under the pretence of showing him the long typewritten list, her long, silky black hair entwining itself over his arm as she bent slightly towards him. 'I'm very tired; it was a long journey; I thought I'd go straight to bed if that's all right.'

'Of course.' His voice was cool now and his eyes cold. 'I'll see you tomorrow morning, then.'

'Yes.' She increased the smile to hundred-watt proportions as she allowed her gaze to settle on Lala's smooth, feline features. 'Goodnight.' It would have been polite to add that she had been pleased to meet her but the hypocrisy was too much.

Not so for Lala, it would appear. 'Goodnight.' The brunette's smile was radiant now but the almond eyes looked straight through Louisa. 'It is so nice to have met you.'

Louisa left the room with head held high and legs steady but she paused in the massive empty hall, her gaze flickering over the huge feathery palms, exquisite vase and life-size statue of a young maiden with slim arms uplifted to her long, flowing hair in one shadowed corner. Even she could recognise that it was ancient and wildly expensive, and the whole house was full of treasures like this. It was another world of opulence and wealth beyond her wildest dreams and she had to admit that Lala, or someone like her, would fit in beautifully, whereas she. . . She caught herself sharply. She had been mad out there in the courtyard for just a few brief, crazy moments but it wouldn't happen again. She bit down on her lower lip until she could taste blood. She had burnt her fingers with this man several times now and here, in his own little empire, he would be even more dangerous, as this evening had proved. How many Lalas were there anyway?

He would be interested in nothing more lasting than a brief affair, a little entertainment; she had known it all along deep in her heart. How could she have forgotten? How could she? As she thought of their lovemaking, the caresses she had allowed. . . No, not allowed. Her mind refused to accept anything less than the bitter truth. Encouraged, wanted, enjoyed. . .

Well, never again. She nodded to herself slowly as she walked up the massive open winding staircase, which was regal and majestic in polished wood. Never again. And if she forgot, if she was so criminally foolish as to forget, the searing pain in her heart that was burning her chest would remind her.

'I will brand you, brand you as mine. . .' His words beat a rhythm in her head as she reached the lovely airy room on the second floor that was hers. Yes, he would brand her all right if she allowed it, and the brand would sear her skin, eating through her flesh day by day, week by week, until at last, when he left her, it would be a great ugly hole that would destroy her very sanity. . .

CHAPTER SEVEN

'READY?' Melik smiled at her over the traditional breakfast-table laid with white cheese, black olives, hard-boiled eggs, pots of golden honey and tubs of cherry and plum jam and huge mounds of fresh Turkish bread, still warm from the oven. 'The imam, the Muslim priest, will be leaving the bride's house soon and I would like to visit before the day begins in earnest.'

Louisa drained her small glass of tea before she answered, her face bland. She had grown to like the Turkish tea now, much lighter-coloured than the strong English brew she was used to, but when drunk neat without milk and just a little sugar to taste she had found it could be remarkably refreshing. 'I thought I came here to work while you attended to business? The first I heard of this wedding was last night when Lala——'

'I said I had business at my home and the wedding is business of a sort,' Melik said smoothly, his eyes narrowing at the look on her face. 'Obviously while I am here other business matters will crop up, as you will discover by the intrusion of that wonderful instrument the telephone.'

'But——'

'What business I choose to deal with in the confines of my own estate is not your concern, surely?' Now his eyes were ice-cold.

'Absolutely right.' She met him glare for glare. 'But

a wedding is a social occasion and there is no way I have to join in that, is there? So if you'll excuse me I'll work here until——'

'The hell you will.' His voice was quiet and even and controlled. 'I take it this unconcealed antagonism is my answer to the questions I proposed last night before Lala entered "where angels fear to tread"?'

'I wasn't aware of any questions and I'm sure Lala is no angel,' she said coldly, regretting the last part of the remark as soon as the words left her lips but unable to draw them back.

'You weren't aware. . .' He let his voice die away as he rose slowly, his big, lean body magnificent in black jeans that hugged his hips in a way guaranteed to make any female heart between the ages of nine and ninety beat a little faster, the black denim shirt he wore open at the neck to reveal his muscular tanned throat. 'I see. Well, you will accompany me to the wedding festival, all of it, whether you like it or not,' he said icily, his eyes flashing sparks of green fire. 'It would be considered a grave insult if you did not. And I told you I want your hair loose,' he added autocratically.

'I want it tidy.' She eyed him defiantly although her legs were trembling under the sanctuary of the table.

'This is ridiculous.' As his expression changed and a gentler look warmed his face she tensed painfully. 'I do not wish to fight with you, Louisa.'

'Then let me go back to Istanbul,' she said flatly. 'I can't see that I am needed here and——'

'Enough!' She had pushed him too far; she could see it in the way his teeth had ground together, a muscle jumping at the side of his mouth. 'You will be ready to leave in twenty minutes.'

'And my hair?' She didn't know what little devil was

goading her this morning but it had long black hair and sensual almond-shaped eyes that had been laughing at her all through the long, restless night.

'Do what you want with your hair,' he snarled softly. 'Cut it all off, shave your head if you like, I am past caring. Just be down here in twenty minutes in modest clothing with your mouth shut. Is that understood?'

'Perfectly.'

'Right.'

The village where the bride's parents' house was situated was just a few miles away, but as they travelled down the steep unmade road just opposite the huge gates to Melik's estate she began to feel as though she had stepped back in time, a feeling that was intensified as Melik's Range Rover bumped into the tiny market town.

Peasant women, dressed in brightly printed baggy trousers and cotton scarves, their weather-roughened faces bronzed and lined by constant exposure to the sun, sat squatting beside their roughly constructed stalls holding eggs, fruit, goat's cheese and a mass of assorted fresh vegetables.

A group of old men were sitting in companionable harmony in the small café whose doors were wide open, puffing contentedly on their hubble-bubble pipes as they enjoyed a game of backgammon, two young children wandered by leading an elderly sheep on a piece of string and a host of pigeons were ambling about the cobbles, pecking at this and that as their heads nodded busily. It was a scene that hadn't altered for centuries and was all the more poignant after the mad whirl of Istanbul.

'The priest will have left by now,' Melik said tightly as they drew up outside a small flat-roofed house about which several fat and contented chickens were searching for food. 'The family expect me to come today and they know I have a guest. You need do and say very little except smile and nod. They speak no English.' He glanced at her face fleetingly. 'And don't look so nervous; they are just ordinary peasant folk, for goodness' sake, the salt of the earth. The festivities start tomorrow.'

The tiny house was spotlessly clean and packed full with relatives when they entered although it was immediately clear to Louisa, in spite of her lack of Turkish, that Melik even outshone the bride. They seemed ridiculously pleased that he had made the effort to visit and the women, the palms of their hands and their fingertips reddened with henna to bring good luck, immediately enveloped her in the inevitable hospitality that characterised this friendly race.

It was late morning when they left and by then Louisa was quite exhausted with smiling, the muscles of her face aching with the effort.

'They liked you.' Melik's voice was expressionless as the powerful engine urged the Range Rover up the incline away from the village.

'Did they?' She felt a small glow of pleasure that eased the ache in her heart for a few seconds. There had been something unbearably painful in seeing him with his own kind, assured, comfortable, totally at ease be it in the confines of a small peasant house or in the cut and thrust of the modern Western world in which he normally lived. She wanted. . . She didn't know *what* she wanted!

Melik was cool and aloof for the rest of the day and evening, working alone in his study most of the afternoon after giving Louisa some data to compile into neat notes and phone through to Mrs Jones. She felt desolate and abandoned and miserable but forced herself to work slowly, checking her work several times as her mind wandered. Dinner was a subdued affair with Melik very distant and correct and Louisa feeling as though a knife was twisting in her insides every time she glanced up and caught the hooded eyes.

The next day dawned cool but dry, a light wind lowering the temperature a good few degrees as the day progressed. They were due to join the celebrations in the afternoon and Louisa would have given the world not to go. She was still trying to think of an excuse when Melik walked through to the small room at the back of the house where she was working on some notes for Lectron.

'Ready?' He didn't smile and her stomach jolted as she glanced up. He was dressed simply but smartly in loose black cotton trousers and matching shirt, a heavy jacket in a dark jade-green causing the green flecks in his eyes to shine out with more colour than usual.

'Do you really want me to come?' she asked hesitantly as she half rose to her feet. 'I'm not being awkward,' she added hastily as his eyes frosted, 'but I don't know anyone and I shan't understand what's going on. . .'

He eyed her intently for a few long minutes and then relaxed visibly, walking across to sit on the side of the long, low desk on which she had been working, which brought his hard-muscled body within inches of her eyeline.

'Yesterday the priest came to the bride's house to perform a short ceremony that included prayer and an explanation of the marriage vows,' he said quietly, his eyes tight on hers. 'Today there are parties, a separate one for the men and another for the women, and don't worry——' he had noticed the panic in her large brown eyes '—Safiye and her daughters will be there with you and Lala too, I should imagine.'

The thought was curiously uncomforting.

'We will dance and eat, and most of the men will imbibe vast quantities of raki that may well cause a few problems later on.' His voice was wry. 'Especially as the custom for guns to be brought out and fired at the night sky needs a steady hand and a sober mind. The bride's female relatives will wash her and dress her in veils and numerous layers of colourful cloth in time for the groom's friends to arrive at the house and ask for her hand, which is refused until a gift is given to her family. Understand so far?' She nodded slowly, her senses absorbing the intoxicatingly delicious smell of him and the way his muscled thighs stretched the black cloth over his hips.

'The groom climbs on to the roof of the house and breaks an earthenware jug which signifies the scaring away of evil spirits at such an important time. That is the point where many a bride's wedding night has had to be delayed through broken bones,' he added drily, a dark amusement in his eyes, 'and finally, flushed and excited and lovely in her wedding finery, the bride is led to her new home and the bedroom where she awaits her husband. And then—— But perhaps you can imagine from there?' he asked mockingly as she flushed a deep rich scarlet at the dark glitter in his gaze. He smiled slowly at her nod. 'You will be fine; you will enjoy it, I promise.' He reached out and stroked her cheek for a brief moment, his eyes strangely guarded. 'Safiye will take care of you until I am with you again.'

In other circumstances, in another age, that sentence

could have meant something so different, she thought shakily as she followed him out to the Range Rover slowly. But this was here and now and it meant nothing beyond the polite consideration any Turkish host would feel for a visitor in his home. And she had to master this feeling that had been growing on her lately, the longing to have someone on whom she could lean, someone to protect her, someone to show her what it really meant to be a woman, to love her — She caught herself angrily. Someone? Why lie to herself? It was Melik who haunted her dreams, but only because of this strange physical attraction they had for each other which would die the death of all such fleeting emotions. It was shallow, insubstantial, it *was*.

Amazingly, wonderfully, the next few hours proved surprisingly enjoyable. Safiye and her daughters remained glued to her side like obedient sentries, the Turkish women in the village opened up their hearts to her and made her welcome in a way that brought a lump to her throat, and the wonderful food, spread over a huge old wooden table that had been scrubbed to pristine cleanliness before being spread with a beautifully woven cloth hand-embroidered with butterflies, flowers and woodland scenes, was incredibly good. The party was in the open air and from the sounds at the other end of the village so was the men's. The bride was beautiful, from the top of her carefully oiled hair covered with a veil and tiny tinkling coins to the bottom of her henna-covered feet, and when later they had led her to the tiny cottage she was to occupy with her new husband at the very edge of the village Louisa felt a twist to her heart that had the tears pricking at the back of her eyes. Would Melik's eventual bride keep to the old ways?

Lala hadn't joined the party until almost the last minute just before the groom's friends came to the bride's house, and Louisa tried to push the unworthy thought aside that the beautiful Turkish girl had been waiting until the men were in evidence again before she made an appearance.

'Hello, Louisa.' The perfectly pitched voice was as cold as ice, the slanted eyes openly hostile. 'You came, then?'

'Yes.' Louisa stared at her warily, sensing that Lala wouldn't hold back on what she was clearly longing to say now that Melik wasn't present. She had also chosen an opportune moment to speak alone with Louisa without the threat of being overheard. In all the excitement of the traditional bargaining in front of them no one was listening to their conversation.

'I wondered if you would.' Lala smoothed what must have been a wildly expensive silk dress over her shapely hips. 'You are an executive in this English firm that Melik is involved with? A manager maybe?' The black eyes were tight and narrowed.

'Not exactly.' Louisa's hackles rose at the imperious tone.

'No?' Lala moved even closer until the heavy, clinging musky scent she wore seemed to permeate Louisa's skin. 'What, then?' she asked arrogantly. 'A personal assistant, secretary?'

'I'm just involved in the project,' Louisa said carefully, 'that's all.' She looked around for Safiye and her daughters but they were totally engrossed in the groom's friends' laughing chatter with the bride's parents, the rest of the men beginning to come down the main road in a noisy, shouting, dancing crowd. Damn! She didn't want an argument, however obscure, with this unpleasant, disagreeable young woman. In fact she didn't want any contact with her at all if she could help it.

'That is all?' The biting contempt in Lala's voice was too vitriolic to ignore and suddenly Louisa forgot all about appeasement as her quick temper rose to the bait. 'You think I am a foolish woman, is that it?' The slanted eyes narrowed still further into black slits. 'Well, I have, as you say, been around quite a bit and I know the score. Melik has never brought a woman to his home before; why you?'

'Why don't you ask *him*?' Louisa said coldly. 'And I don't doubt for a minute that you've done the rounds, Lala.'

'I shall ask.' Lala shook her head slightly so that the long gold earrings made up of hundreds of tiny little balls on thin gold threads jangled in the night air. 'That is *exactly* what I intend to do.' She glared at Louisa as though she hated her.

'Good.' Louisa stared at her coolly, her mouth straight. 'He'll be here shortly so if you'll excuse me. . .' She moved the few steps that brought her to Safiye's side determinedly. If Lala thought she was going to engage in a verbal cat fight she had another think coming! She wouldn't lower herself to Lala's standards.

When Melik joined them a few minutes later Lala was already clinging like a limpet to his arm where she remained with sweet-faced determination. Louisa was conscious of herself talking, laughing, behaving normally, while all the time it was as if she were a spectator watching a play, a painfully bad play. She couldn't have put a name to the feeling that was burning her up inside but she recognised anger as one of the ingredients, that and a hot cutting humiliation when she thought of how near she had been to succumbing completely, yielding totally to Melik's will after some clever lovemaking that he had no doubt practised countless times before and which clearly meant absolutely nothing to him.

'Am I being invited for a nightcap?' Lala's voice was laughingly provocative as, the bride safely hidden away with her new husband, the festivities began to break up and everyone returned to his or her own home.

'Of course.' Just for a moment Louisa thought she caught a thread of irritation in Melik's politely cool voice but dismissed it immediately as imagination. 'Do you have transport?'

'My jeep is parked behind the square.' The sloe eyes fluttered as they rested on Melik's darkly bronzed face in the dancing shadows of skittering moonlight. 'Would you drive for me? It's so dark and it's beginning to rain. . .'

It was. How convenient, Louisa thought caustically. What would the excuse have been to get Melik all to herself if the weather had stayed fine? It was too dark? She was too tired?

'No problem; Tegrul can drive the Range Rover; it was packed a bit tight with the six of us earlier anyway. Louisa, you will come with us?' It was an order couched in a question and suddenly everything in Louisa rebelled. Did he seriously think she was going to travel in the back of Lala's jeep, where she would undoubtedly be put like a sack of potatoes, listening to the two of them billing and cooing while pretending to enjoy being the proverbial green gooseberry? Well, thanks but no, thanks! This was way beyond the call of duty.

'Don't worry.' She forced a cold smile to her face,

knowing that outright defiance in front of Lala and the Turkish villagers drifting around would cause a scene that would be embarrassing for everyone concerned. 'Safiye was in the middle of explaining a few of the meanings behind such a traditional wedding so I'll go with them. See you at the house.'

She gave Melik no time to react, walking over to Tegrul and Safiye who were standing beside the Range Rover and telling Tegrul that Melik wanted him for a moment. 'Tegrul's driving us back,' she explained shortly to Safiye. 'He needs the keys.' As she turned slightly she met an angry gold gaze for one blinding moment which she returned with scathing thoroughness before Tegrul joined them again and they climbed into the Range Rover. She didn't look back once.

On reaching the house she flew up to her room as though she had wings on her feet, locking the door hastily before running a warm shower in the *en suite* and, after discarding her clothes in a heap on the floor, stepping under the cascading flow of water with her eyes shut and her head pounding. She hated him! She really hated him. Letting Lala hang over him with such a total display of wantonness. 'Overbearing, conceited swine. . .' She stared viciously at the streaming shower door as she opened hot eyes. 'He thinks he's God's gift to womankind! Well, not *this* woman!'

She heard the banging on the bedroom door long before she stepped out of the shower but ignored it for as long as she could, and then, when she felt as though the wood was going to give way, she hastily wrapped her hair in a short hand-towel before pulling on her full-length towelling robe and knotting the belt tightly round her waist with fingers that shook.

'Yes?' Seizing a moment in between blows, she kept

her voice cold and strong with superhuman effort. 'Is there someone there?'

'Is there. . .?' She heard Melik's furiously incredulous voice die away with a fleeting stab of satisfaction. 'Open this damn door, *now!*'

'Why?' She could hear the sound of his angry panting behind the door and for a moment her heart pounded with fear.

'Louisa, I have no intention of standing here and talking through wood. Open the door.'

'No.' She heard herself defy him with mounting horror. 'I've just had a shower and I'm getting ready for bed. I've no ——'

As the door burst open and Melik cannoned into the room she literally froze with fear, her eyes huge as she took in his glowering face and blazing eyes that were piercing in his rage. 'Melik ——'

'Don't you "Melik" me,' he ground out savagely through clenched teeth. 'I should think everyone in this whole area, let alone my household, has heard me banging on that door.'

'Where's Lala?'

'Where the hell do you think she is?' he snarled softly. 'Downstairs waiting for you to join us for a drink.' His body was almost rigid with the control he was forcing on himself. 'I don't know what you're playing at but I want you dressed and downstairs within five seconds.'

'No.' A tiny separate piece of her mind was looking on with absolute amazement but something stronger than herself and him was driving her on. 'I'm not coming down, Melik.'

'You're not. . .' For the second time in as many minutes his voice faded away in incredulous fury, and she saw him close his eyes for a brief moment as he took a long deep breath, lowering his head before raising it again to look straight into her terrified eyes. 'Why?' It was one word but all the more frightening in the icy cold way it was delivered.

'Because I don't want to.' She would never, ever give him the satisfaction of even suspecting for a minute that she was jealous, because she wasn't, she *wasn't*.

'You don't want to,' he repeated flatly. 'I really don't believe I am having this conversation.' He raked back a lock of hair that had fallen across his brow as he had forced the door open and glared at her again, the cool, suave businessman whom she had known for so long and who was completely in control of himself and everything else having totally vanished. 'Am I permitted to know the reason for this sudden aversion to my drawing-room?' he asked scathingly.

'It's not a crime to want to go to bed, is it?' she said weakly. 'I really don't think —'

'Louisa, no one has ever made me as angry as I feel right now,' he said slowly as his hard jawline tightened into pure granite, 'and although I'm trying, for both our sakes, to remain calm and reasonable you are making it damnably hard.' As he had been speaking the towel had begun to slide off the soft, silky curls beneath it and as it fell on to her shoulders and the mass of riotously golden hair sprung round her face his eyes darkened still further. 'Now are you going to get dressed by yourself or do I have to do it for you?'

'You just try it!' She took a step backwards, clutching the ends of the belt to her as she spoke. 'If you lay one finger on me I'll scream this place down.'

'And who do you think would come running to your

rescue?' he asked icily, his eyes flashing at her dogged rebelliousness.

'Tegrul, Safiye. . .' She raised her head proudly. 'Someone.'

'Someone.' He smiled slowly, a cruel snarl of a smile that had no amusement whatsoever in its depths. 'It would be more than their lives are worth and they know it.' He straightened, his shoulders big and broad against the dim lamp that was lighting the room and his hair as black as midnight. 'Now, Lala is waiting down there, no doubt wondering what the hell is going on, and you are going to come down and behave like a normal, well behaved young woman however difficult such an unusual piece of play-acting may be for you. Do you understand me?'

'I'm not.' She took another step backwards as she spoke, her eyes huge in the whiteness of her face. 'You can't make me.'

'Louisa, *making* you would be the least of my problems,' he said throatily. 'I haven't the faintest idea what this is all about but it stops now.'

'You're such a bully,' she whispered faintly as the realisation that he might, he just might, force her to go downstairs like a whipped puppy and face Lala for what was left of the evening dawned on her consciousness. 'I hate you, I really do.'

The flash of something—for a crazy moment she thought it was pain—that seared across his face seemed to shatter the last of his self-control. As he reached out for her she found she was frozen with fear, her mind and body numb as he lifted her up and carried her across the room to where her clothes lay scattered on the floor.

'Put them on.'

'Never.'

He threw her on to the bed with such force that she bounced upwards, the robe jerking open before she grabbed the sides in a vain attempt to cover her nakedness from his gaze.

'Damn you. . .' As he joined her on the bed she was aware of two things — his face torn with conflicting emotions of rage and desire and her own traitorous body that leapt into immediate life as he moved over her, his lips hot on her face.

'You won't be content until you break me, will you?'

It was more the passionate response of her body to his than anything that had gone before that had her fighting him like the small tigress he had accused her so often of being. She knew, if she let it, that the weakening, liquefying effect his lovemaking aroused would soon turn her body compliant and submissive beneath his, that his vastly superior experience would overcome all her resistance until she was quivering and shaking under his caresses. . .like before. *And it couldn't happen again.*

'Louisa. . .' He groaned her name against her flesh, his overwhelming hunger evident in every hard, aroused line of his body, his lips rough and demanding as they burnt over her skin like fire. And to her dismay, to her utter shame, she found that his passion was igniting a desire in her that terrified her.

She wanted him, she wanted his hands on her body, she wanted him to be the first one to possess her utterly, the only one. She wanted it because she *loved* him. The thought froze her beneath him but, caught up in his own need, he didn't notice for a moment. That was why the sight of Lala touching him, holding him, inviting him to take her with every glance, every movement, had hurt so badly. It wasn't physical desire only that had bonded her to this man from the first moment she had laid eyes on him. There had been something, even then, that had reached far beyond the mere outward form.

And the other women. . .that he had had in the past, that he *would have* in the future. . .that was what had been eating her up for the last few weeks until she had turned into a creature she hardly recognised. And there was nothing she could do about it, nothing at all, because the bottom line was that he didn't want her, not all of her, not in the way she cared for him. That was one thing she *had* known all along. The years of being alone, of childhood rejection and betrayal, had prepared her for that knowledge at least.

As the tears seeped hot and fierce beneath her closed eyelids she felt his body stiffen, his hands and mouth still for a long moment before he moved off her in one swift movement.

'Louisa?' She felt he was standing by the bed but couldn't open her eyes, couldn't move. 'Don't cry.' He said something harsh and violent under his breath in his own language, his voice strained and tight as he drove his fist into his hand.

And then he was gone, the door shutting behind him with a softness that was deafening. And she was alone. More alone than she had ever been in her life.

CHAPTER EIGHT

'LOUISA?' She had crawled into bed after he had gone, burying down into the covers like a small animal trying to hide, lying in still misery for long, painful minutes, but now the voice outside the door had her jolting bolt upright, her hands across her mouth.

'I have sent Lala home but I must talk with you. You have my word that I will not touch you.' The hard male voice faltered and then continued. 'You have nothing to fear, I promise you.'

She sat frozen and breathless before answering, her mind stunned. 'Come in.'

He didn't turn on the light, for which she was thankful, moving across to the side of the bed slowly in the muted darkness. 'There is nothing I can say to absolve my actions of their outrage, nothing at all, and to ask you to forgive such a betrayal of hospitality would be the final insult.' She listened to his voice, cold and steady now, with a faint feeling of disbelief. Was that all he was concerned about? That he had in some way offended one of the many social laws in which this country was steeped?

'I need to be here for a few days and I also need you to deal with the business side of things with Lectron. If you feel that you cannot stay, that you want to return immediately to Istanbul, it can be arranged.' She bit her lip tightly in the darkness. He was so cold, so remote. 'The decision must be yours. All I can say is that if you decide to stay such an occurrence will not happen again. On that you have my word. Think it over and let me have your decision in the morning, unless you are decided now?'

The air was heavy and silent for a few moments and then she forced herself to speak, her voice amazingly normal in view of the churning inside. 'I'll see you in the morning.'

'Very well.' There was another tense silence, as though he wanted to say more, and then she heard him moving across the room and the door snapped quietly into place. He had only been visible as a big dark shadow but even so, in spite of being unable to see the expression on his face, she had longed to reach out to him. She was weak. The thought stung a little but not enough to hurt. All her senses, all her emotions were tied up in the devastating fact she had just learnt about herself. She loved him. He was the last man on earth she would have chosen to love but choice had got very little to do with it. It was crazy, emotional suicide, but she knew as the long, sleepless night dragged on that she would walk through live coals if it could make him feel even a fraction of what she felt for him.

When the first cold light of day began to filter into her room it was to the accompaniment of hard, driving rain against the window, which in a strange way was more comforting than sunshine. She padded across to the large full-length window and pulled aside the soft, filmy curtains and wooden shutters to peer out into the grey sky. It was almost torrential, the stone floor of the balcony an inch deep and the bedraggled pots of plants looking as though they would be swept away any moment.

What was she going to say to him? As the pale pearly light washed over her strained face and tangled hair she shook herself irritably, her expression one of bitter self-contempt. She *knew* what she was going to say to him; she had known it since the last visit to her room when he had given her a way of staying on here with him without losing face. It was madness, the worst form of self-torture, but. . .she wanted to be near to him even if it was unbearably painful. She leant her forehead against the cold, hard glass. The affection and warm gratitude she had felt for Oliver was nothing like this agonisingly fierce emotion that was making her feel physically ill. Suddenly the knowledge didn't seem like a betrayal to his memory any more. She had loved him in a brotherly, gentle way, a comfortable, almost sexless affection perhaps, but she *had* still loved him and he had been content with that. If she had married him their life together would have been one of nine-to-five routine with maybe cocoa and a good book at night and the traditional two point four children in due course. And she would have been content. Not exactly happy, not fulfilled, but content.

And Melik? Her heart pounded into her throat. It was crazy even to consider what it would be like if he loved her, because he never would, but life with him would be. . .paradise. Paradise and hell. Paradise when he was with her, loving her, reassuring her, and hell when he was away. Because he wouldn't lie. She knew that. If he had other women she would either have to leave or look the other way and either choice would be impossible, loving him as she did. So it was better he didn't love her. The ethereal reflection in the glass mocked her. *It was, it was.*

'Louisa?' He rose swiftly as she walked into the breakfast-room two hours later, outwardly perfectly composed if a little white but inwardly in such turmoil that the sight of him nearly caused her to break down. The memories were so vivid, so strong, she could still feel the taste of him as he had held her in his arms. . .

'I want to say something and then it's over.' She stood in front of her chair and looked straight into the hard, tawny eyes, noticing as she did so that his face was a little grey, his mouth strained.

'Over?' For a moment she thought he had gone a shade paler but it was the strange half-light from the appalling weather outside as the wind drove the splintering needles of rain with such force against the windows that they shook.

'Yes, over, I don't want it mentioned again.' She stared at him steadily, the effort it took making her legs tremble. 'Last night was a mistake, on both our parts.' She took a deep breath as his face remained curiously still. 'When I looked back over it all I realised I might have been a bit unreasonable —— ' She held up her hand as he went to speak. 'No, let me finish, please. We were both tired, overwrought, and it was a one-off. Yes?'

'Louisa —— '

'And the only way I can stay here and finish the job you've asked me to do is to pretend it never happened, to go back twenty-four hours if you like.'

'Pretend it never happened?' There was a muscle working in his jaw that spoke volumes. 'You think I can pretend it never happened? That I didn't hold you in my arms, kiss —— ?'

'It's either that or I leave today.' The silence went on and on, but she couldn't, she just couldn't have a post-mortem on all the buts and wherefores when her heart was so raw and this new knowledge still had the power to terrify her half to death. 'I don't blame you,

I don't blame myself; it was just one of those things but I want to wipe it out of my memory.'

'I see.' He had the look of a man who had been punched hard in the stomach. 'I frightened you that badly? You found my touch so repugnant?'

There was nothing she could say without making a fool of herself and bursting into tears, and after a pregnant silence broken only by the hurtling raindrops he nodded slowly, his eyes bleak. 'So be it. We will continue as before. I have a pile of papers waiting for my attention so if you'll excuse me. . .?' And he left abruptly, his shoulders tight and his head facing straight ahead.

Twenty-four hours later a minor catastrophe occurred with the English side of the partnership which demanded long hours, countless phone calls and major restructuring with one of the components, but amazingly, at the end of four days of working almost sixteen hours a day, Louisa found their relationship, at least on a superficial level, was healed. They were able to talk comfortably, smile, and even exchange a wry comment or two, although she felt, at least, that the undercurrents were fiercely tense.

She was still thinking along these lines on the evening of the fifth day when Melik appeared in the doorway of her small room, strewn with papers, and smiled lazily as he glanced round at the disarray. 'You were such a tidy little thing when I first took you on,' he said ruefully as the tawny gaze swept over a heap of reports spread across the spare desk in flowing disorder. 'I'm a bad influence, am I not?'

You just don't know, she thought painfully with dark humour as she smiled brightly, her voice light. 'Not at all.'

'I think so.' He paused, and as she still looked up at him spoke a little abruptly. 'There is a dancer I would like you to see at a little restaurant I know, a rather special place.'

'I don't think ——'

'She rarely dances now,' he continued as though she hadn't interrupted, 'but when she does it is quite magical. She is an old friend and knows I am here for a few days. It would be impolite not to go.'

'I see.' Her pulses had leapt into crazy life at this, their first conversation for days about anything other than work, and every treacherous bone in her body was reaching out to the chance of being with him even though she would regret it, perhaps bitterly. But she had the rest of her life to dwell on such things and more and more, as the hours and days had gone by, she had begun to wonder if maybe, somehow, she had misunderstood about Lala, maybe projected her own doubts and fears into a situation that was quite innocent, at least on Melik's part. She had never felt so miserable and confused in all her life, one minute firmly convinced that all was deep blackness and the next sensing a little chink of light at the end of the tunnel.

She had done some hard thinking, faced some tough issues over the last few lonely nights as she'd lain sleepless and heartsore in her bed, and slowly, reluctantly, had come to the conclusion that she had never given him the chance to show her what he was really like; she had been too busy holding him firmly at arm's length. Dared she *take* a chance?

'I've arranged for my plane to pick us up at seven o'clock,' he continued expressionlessly. 'Is that enough time for you to get ready?'

'I haven't said I'll come yet!' All the finer feelings and tender heart-searchings fled in the face of his presumption. 'I thought we'd —'

'And it will be evening dress.' She opened her mouth to argue further but something in the warm, smoky gaze stopped her. He was looking at her in a way he hadn't done for days and it stopped her heart beating. 'Now you have precisely. . .' he checked the gold watch on his wrist with casual authority '. . .an hour and twenty minutes to get ready. OK?'

It wasn't but she nodded anyway.

Exactly one hour and nineteen minutes later she took one last long look in the full-length mirror in critical appraisal, seeing only the beautiful close-fitting and low-cut evening dress in dark jade silk that had cost her a month's salary some time ago, the small dark green studs in her ears of exactly the same hue and the carefully upswept hair that she had allowed to fall in tiny tendrils round her neck and face. The huge, heavily lashed velvet brown eyes, tiny straight nose and wide, full lips she glanced over in perfunctory indifference; her beauty had never brought her happiness and she had learnt long ago to place no value on its superficial appeal.

A minute later as she walked down the long, winding staircase and Melik moved out to watch her, his golden eyes stunned with appreciation, she felt, for the first time in her life, a faint stirring of pleasure that she wasn't ugly.

'You look very lovely.' His voice was low and soft and tender and her nerves curled with delight as he reached out a hand and touched the nape of her neck where a small cluster of golden curls gleamed in the light. 'Do I take it that this is some sort of compromise?' he asked mockingly as he allowed a tiny ringlet to trail over his bronzed finger. 'A halfway house?'

'If you like.' She smiled lightly.

'Oh, I do like,' he said lazily, his eyes glittering hotly. 'I like very much indeed.'

So did she but she wasn't going to tell him that, she thought faintly, as the sight of the big, lean body in full evening dress did crazy things to her equilibrium. He looked very big and very dark and strangely, in spite of the traditional dress, more savage and untamed than she had ever seen him. The powerful set of his shoulders, the long, muscled legs and wide, strong chest were all magnificently accentuated by the austere dark suit and snow-white shirt, and the quiver that began in her lower stomach moved swiftly to the rest of her body.

'Shall we?' As he took her arm she almost jerked away, every nerve so sensitised that even the casual hand on her elbow sent ripples down her back, but she controlled the gesture just in time, smiling coolly and stopping to pull on the light wool coat she had over her arm.

'I don't think so.' He took the coat from her hands and slung it on a nearby table, his eyes bright and glittering. 'Here.'

She had noticed the large package at one side of the stairs but had thought little of it, but now, as he handed her the parcel, she raised enquiring, apprehensive eyes to his. 'What is it?'

'I can assure you it will not bite so you can open it without fear,' he said drily as she held the gift almost at arm's length. His eyes softened as she still stared at him warily. 'You are as refreshing as a sea breeze, my little tigress,' he drawled slowly after a long moment had lingered on the air. 'Most women of my acquaintance would have had that parcel unwrapped in two seconds flat with a pretty thank-you and a hope for more.'

'Would they?' Although the words had been faintly mocking there had been something in the stunningly handsome face that had told her he was not displeased.

As she tore the layers of tissue and the soft, silky peach material draped itself over her arms she looked up quickly, her cheeks scarlet. 'It's the shawl.'

'Indeed it is.' He was watching her carefully, his proud, intelligent face expressionless. 'And if it interests you at all I have never had to wait so long and with such fear and trepidation to give a woman a gift before.' He took the rich, glowing material from her hands as she stood silent and still in front of him and draped it carefully around her shoulders, his touch sensual and warm.

'It's beautiful, Melik, and it's not that I'm unappreciative——'

He turned her round, placing a finger on her lips as he directed the full power of his golden gaze on her face. 'I did not think that for a moment,' he said softly. 'I know exactly what you are, my English rose — warm, lovely, fierce, proud, sensitive. I have said before, you are Turkish under that white skin and golden hair. I just have to find the key to unlock the door that you have closed so tightly but in this I am learning patience. It is not a lesson that comes easy but I am learning it. I will not frighten you again.'

'You didn't——' She stopped abruptly, her head whirling as he placed his lips on hers for a fleeting moment, his mouth warm and firm.

'I am tenacious, Louisa, tenacious and very stubborn, but I do not consider these faults.' His eyes glowed in the darkness of his skin. 'I hold fast to what is mine and I take what I want as long as it does not belong to someone else.'

The Mercedes was waiting as they walked out into the cold, clear air, the storms of the previous days having cleared the last remnants of summer from the atmosphere and replaced it with a crispness that was invigorating and clean.

'Osman will drive us to my airfield where the plane is waiting.' His voice was as cool and as matter-of-fact as if he had just announced that they were popping across to the local supermarket for a basket of provisions. As he helped her into the car and the chauffeur shut the door, his face as impassive as always, Melik reached out and took her hand in his, tracing a circle in one soft palm as he looked deep into her eyes. 'You look breathtakingly beautiful and I am proud to be your escort,' he said softly, his accent very pronounced. 'Enjoy this evening, Louisa; it is my wish that you do so.'

'Thank you. . .' It didn't seem real; none of it seemed real — the short drive to a huge cleared area of land where Melik's small light plane was housed, and then, with Osman at the controls, the brief flight across dark wooded country, the sky a dark midnight-blue blanket wrapped around them and the moon a bright silver ball in the heavens. She tried to concentrate, to take in what was happening, but with Melik warm and solid at her side and his masculine scent of musk on hard male skin it was nearly impossible.

They arrived at a massive, brightly lit enclosure surrounded by a row of tiny blinking lights where a car was waiting to whisk them to the restaurant and as she settled into the back of the stately Bentley she felt utterly bemused at the effortless power of such wealth. It all happened so easily, everything like clockwork, and he had been used to this all his life. She darted a quick glance at his dark face under her eyelashes. When money was no object the impossible became effortlessly simple, the unattainable child's play. It was all so smooth and straightforward for him and if it wasn't he threw some money into the system and it became so. Was that why he had decided he wanted her? She shifted slightly in her seat as she stared out into the dark night. Because he was being thwarted of a possession for once in his life and the challenge appealed? No. She gave her head a mental shake. That would suggest he was petulant, childish, and there was nothing small in this man's make-up. She had to believe that, needed to.

'There it is, the House of the Crescent Moon.' They had driven along a tree-lined avenue for some distance and now the lights that had been in the distance materialised into a huge, fairy-castle type structure of mellow old stone and tall turrets and pillars. The floodlit courtyard filled with expensive cars was surrounded by tiny sparkling fountains with a mass of dark green vegetation beyond in the shadowed darkness that wafted exotic scents into the cool night.

'It's gorgeous.' Louisa looked up at Melik to see the tawny eyes were fixed tight on her face. 'It doesn't look real.'

'Oh, it's real,' he assured her softly. 'The story goes that it was a Genoese fortress fallen sadly into a state of disrepair before the family who owned it, a wealthy Turkish businessman who lived in Istanbul and his seven daughters, decided to transform it into an exclusive hotel and move here. They have the occasional floor show but only the very best is allowed; their reputation is of the highest calibre.'

The huge, high-ceilinged room that they were ushered into after stepping through the massive nail-studded arched doors into a gracious lobby was spectacularly beautiful, and as they were shown to their candlelit table she saw that the discreetly scattered tables and chairs were grouped round a large, slightly raised platform on which a group of musicians with long black hair and brilliantly coloured flowing robes were playing soft Eastern music under the subdued glow of the spotlights.

As they were seated Melik spoke in rapid Turkish to the waiter hovering deferentially at his elbow, who immediately disappeared into the semi-gloom with a smile and a nod. 'A bottle of champagne while we decide what to eat,' Melik explained in answer to her raised eyebrows, handing her the elaborate menu and settling back in his seat comfortably.

The waiter returned almost immediately with a bottle of vintage champagne in an ice-bucket and a big smile. Bollinger. No wonder he was smiling. This evening must be costing Melik a small fortune. Was this the final assault on her defences? An attack to storm the bastion of her heart with no holds barred and using every weapon at his disposal — and he had a few. . .

She pushed the unworthy and disturbing thoughts aside and sipped the ice-cold champagne that tasted of every fragrant summer she had known. 'It's delicious.' She smiled carefully. And if this was the grand seduction scene? Would she mind? A few days ago she would have been so sure of her answer but now. . . Now she wasn't sure of anything.

As she glanced round the room she saw that the clientele matched the décor — rich, elegant and very, very exclusive.

'Would you like me to order?' The menu had been in Turkish, French and English but she had found the English as indecipherable as the other languages.

'Yes, please.' She raised grateful eyes to his face.

'How about *Mantarli borek* for starters?' he asked quietly. 'It's a little pie of flaky pastry stuffed with mushrooms and cheese.'

'That sounds lovely.'

It was, and when washed down with the clean, fragrant wine doubly so. The grilled swordfish steaks accompanied by a spicy salad and savoury rice were equally delicious.

'The rich resources of the Black Sea yield a tasty bounty, do they not?' Melik smiled warmly and as she went to reply, her eyes sparkling with the pleasure his company and the good food had induced, Louisa saw his face freeze with disbelief as he glanced over her shoulder.

'*Hayir*, I do not believe it.'

'What's wrong?'

As she half turned and met Lala's cool, slanted gaze from the table across the other side of the large room her own face froze. Lala? The subdued lighting made it difficult to be sure. Melik lifted a hand in brief salute to which Lala replied with a bright little smile and wave. 'What a coincidence.' He turned back to Louisa with a slow shake of his head and she took a grain of comfort from the fact that he didn't look overly delighted to see the luscious brunette. 'This place is not usually so crowded.' The joke fell flat as she stared at him in amazement. He didn't really believe it *was* a coincidence, did he? Here they were in the middle of nowhere, at the sort of place that she would imagine it wouldn't be untoward to see dukes and duchesses, and lo and behold there was little Lala sitting comfortably in the corner like a big black spider. And she had noticed the wary narrowing of the beautiful eyes when she had first turned round and then the quick flash of relief that had shimmered across Lala's face when Melik had acknowledged her. Somehow she had found out they were going to be here tonight and with all her will-power and considerable wealth behind her the lovely brunette had decided they would not be alone.

'Did Safiye book the table?' Louisa asked quietly as Melik refilled their glasses with the sparkling liquid.

'Yes.' He glanced at her in surprise. 'Why do you ask?'

So that was it. She had heard Safiye talking to Lala on the phone that morning and had assumed the Turkish woman had phoned regarding estate business as she did occasionally, the two plantations being side by side, but although that might have been the excuse she would bet her bottom dollar that Lala had been checking up on Melik, knowing Louisa was still in residence.

Louisa shrugged gracefully. It was no use suggesting that Lala had engineered this episode on purpose. She would deny it and Melik would believe the Turkish girl; he had known her all his life after all. But why did men have to be so *blind*? 'No reason.'

As she expected Lala took about thirty seconds to make her way over to their table, her long, slim body encased in a dress of black silk that was remarkable for the lack of material holding it together, the plunging, strapless top, cut-away sides and huge slits either side of the pencil-slim skirt making her olive skin gleam and shine with sleek sinuousness as she weaved to their side.

'How amazing. . .' She stood just to one side of Melik who had risen at her approach, the slanted black eyes opened wide in surprised innocence and her long neck graceful and poised and seeming almost too slender for the weight of hair that was coiled in a gleaming mass on top of her head and threaded with tiny silver pearls. 'I just couldn't believe my eyes a moment ago. . .' She put a hand to her hair in a feminine little gesture that accentuated the silky swell of her breasts in the low-cut dress, and raised her eyes to Melik beseechingly. 'You must come and join us; it's Father's birthday next week and this is my surprise to him and Mother, a spur-of-the-moment thing.'

Surprise, surprise, Louisa thought balefully. How transparent, how utterly transparent.

'Perhaps later.' Melik smiled down at her indulgently and Louisa felt such a hot stab of undiluted anger that it surprised her into keeping silent.

'Please do.' Lala put the tips of her fingers on his arm, her hand tiny against his muscled bulk and a diamond bracelet that would have paid Louisa's salary for a year flashing on her slim wrist. 'Mother and Father would love it and they haven't met Louisa yet.' She flashed a hard smile at Louisa as she spoke. 'And I suppose you'll be leaving us soon?' It was said with such gentleness, such sweetness, that for a second the only emotion Louisa felt was one of sickness at such hypocrisy, and then she found the strength from somewhere to look the other girl straight in the face, their eyes meeting and locking in a tight scrutiny that was all the more deadly for its silence.

'What makes you suppose that?' Louisa forced herself to smile lightly and take a sip of wine before she
continued, pleased to see that her hands were perfectly
steady as they held the fine crystal goblet. 'I don't think
anything is certain and life has a way of surprising us,
doesn't it?'

As she finished speaking there was an announcement
in Turkish by one of the musicians and even before he
had finished a low ripple of excitement drifted from
table to table. 'I will see you later, then?' Lala brought
her other hand up to Melik's hard face in a fleeting
caress before she left, her rapier-sharp gaze cutting
into Louisa one last time as she glided away, the dark
eyes malevolent and alive with bitter resentment. It
was out-and-out war now, Louisa acknowledged flatly.
Well, so be it.

Immediately after the musician had finished speaking
a low throbbing had begun to vibrate round the room,
and as the spotlight died she noticed several of the men
were extinguishing the candles on their tables until
soon the whole room was steeped in a velvet blackness,
the only thin ray of light filtering from one dusky red
lamp over the middle of the stage. The throbbing
became louder and although the musicians couldn't be
seen she felt as though they were one with their music
as they called forth an almost unbearably poignant
sound, no one instrument dominating another but flute,
drum, zither and pipe combining in an Eastern melody
that pulsed electrifyingly round the darkened room.

Lala's spite, the whole difficult situation, suddenly
faded away like the extinguished candles and Louisa
found she was leaning forward in quivering excitement,
her eyes glued to the tiny red glow and her whole body
tensed and expectant. The rhythm dipped and swayed,

taking the listeners with it, and then as in one flash the light was gone in another it was brighter than before and this time a woman stood in its full glare, her arms raised and her head thrown back, exposing the taut line of her throat and the mass of burnished bronze hair that hung in abandonment almost to her hips.

As she began to move, slowly and with a fluid grace that made her more animal than human, the music almost seemed to be talking to her, leading her into sensual paths of desire that turned her limbs boneless and heightened the impression of a sleek, voluptuous cat, a beautiful golden creature of the night. The thin silk that just covered her breasts crept over her rounded shoulders and down her arms, stopping at her wrists to leave her slim, fine-boned hands free, and her lower body was a mass of weaving, transparent golden veils which she gradually discarded, one by one, until her long legs could be seen in all their pulsing perfection.

She was incredibly supple, moving every muscle, every piece of her flesh in dreamy harmony with the music that gradually began to quicken, to become more urgent. The full, rounded body was plump by Western standards but so liquid, so shockingly erotic, that it was almost painful to watch her.

'Do you understand the story her movements are portraying?' Melik whispered softly by her side, his voice husky and low.

'I think so.' She tore her eyes away from the dancer and turned to him, her pulses racing.

'It is a search for love, for fulfilment.' As she turned back to the writhing figure in the golden light she could feel his eyes burning into her face in the darkness. 'An abandoning of self and reaching out to all that beckons, all that entices. . .'

The music had become more intense now, almost savage, tempting the fluid body on and on as she swayed her hips in an unmistakably sensual invitation that caused the tiny golden coins and tassels edging the diaphanous silk to glitter and dance in the fierce light, all the more intense for the blackness surrounding it.

As the sinuous figure coiled its way among the tables on the other side of the room the spotlight followed her, and Louisa was shocked to see most of the men tucking banknotes into the full cleavage and down into the rounded hips.

'Melik?' Her eyes were wide as she turned back to him. 'What are they doing?'

'It's just the Turkish way of showing appreciation,' he whispered seriously, his straight face belying the leaping amusement in his eyes. 'It's quite in order, I assure you.'

'It is?'

The dancer came nearer and nearer, the music following her in a passionate throbbing that had Louisa feeling quite faint. It was so primitive, so unashamed that all the normal conceptions of what was acceptable seemed totally out of place.

There was a fascination in the dancer's gleaming body, almost an innocence at the total satisfaction with her own sexuality, that was more evocative than anything Louisa had seen before.

She didn't pause at their table although as she passed the heavily made-up eyes smiled at Melik and as Louisa turned to look at him she saw him nod slowly, his eyes tender and his mouth curved in an appreciative smile.

And then, as the music reached an unbearable

crescendo that caused the instruments to wail and strain, the dancer froze in the same position in which she had started, her arms uplifted and open now in an attitude of complete surrender and her face alive with the joy of giving, and a second later the stage was plunged into blackness and the spotlight died.

The darkness, the total silence, was breathtakingly shocking after the intensity of emotion and whirling colour that had gone before, and Louisa felt herself sinking back into her seat with her mind spinning and her senses only half in the real world. The floor show had been more than just a dance, more than a spectacle for culture-starved businessmen and their wives; it had been an insidious persuasion to abandonment, to fleshly love. And Melik had known what it would be like. . .*He had known.*

CHAPTER NINE

THE rest of the entertainment—a snake-charmer complete with deadly-eyed cobras, two young and scantily dressed women who proved to be the most amazing acrobats Louisa had ever seen, contorting their lithe figures into impossible positions, and a soulful-eyed guitarist with a beard and long plaited hair—although excellent, were a definite anticlimax. Added to which with all the candles re-lighted and the stage lit up like a Christmas tree Louisa was painfully conscious of Lala's tight scrutiny from the other side of the room, and it had the effect of making her flesh creep.

'You enjoyed Casia?' Melik asked as the snake-charmer's wailing tune caused one of the cobras to rear out of its basket. 'She is seductive, is she not?'

'Very.' Louisa looked at him carefully. 'How do you know her?'

'I am an old friend of her husband.' It wasn't the reply she was expecting and she gaped at him for a moment in surprise before shutting her mouth with a little snap.

He laughed softly, his eyes mocking and bright. 'I am sorry to disappoint this fertile imagination of yours; no doubt you had the lady designated as one of my many mistresses?'

It was exactly what she had done but she didn't intend to give him the satisfaction of either denying or confirming his suspicions.

'Doesn't he mind her. . .dancing like that?' There

was no censure in her voice, just pure amazement that a Turk, jealous and fiercely proud as a friend of Melik's was bound to be, would allow his wife to enact such an intimate, sensual and suggestive performance that could not fail to raise the temperature of any normal man between the ages of puberty and death.

'He doesn't know.' Melik's voice was soft and even. 'He died when they had only been married three years, leaving her with three children under the age of two — a boy of eighteen months and twin girls who were only a week old when their father was killed in a stupid accident that shouldn't have happened.'

'Oh, Melik. . .' She stared at him aghast, aware from the pain in his voice and the stiffness of his features that his friend's death was still hurting.

'It was an automobile accident,' he continued quietly. 'Just one of those things. I offered to help Casia financially, in fact several people did, but she chose to support herself and her children in the way you have seen her do tonight.

'Now Satuk junior has just passed for university and his sisters are determined to follow him shortly.'

'University?' Her eyes opened wider. The dancer had not looked a day over twenty-one. 'How old is Casia?'

'Not quite the question a lady should ask, but she is thirty-eight; amazing, isn't it?'

'And how!' Louisa breathed. 'And she hasn't married again, got involved with anyone?'

'Not really.' Melik's eyes were quite still now as he held her gaze. 'She loved him, you see, *really* loved him, as he did her. She knows that that sort of emotion only happens once and why should she settle for second best just to make life easier?'

'Do *you* believe that — I mean about it only happening once?' She found she was holding her breath as she waited for his reply.

'I used to believe it probably didn't happen at all until something happened to change my mind,' he said slowly, his eyes locked on her face in such a way that he seemed quite oblivious to his surroundings. 'And then, for the first time, I could understand Casia and her preference for a memory to an inferior replacement.'

'What happened?' she asked breathlessly. 'What changed your mind?' The world stopped, her heart stopped as she waited for his reply.

'Melik, and this must be Louisa? Lala has told us of your visit.' The deep gruff voice at their side brought their heads swivelling round as though they were one to see Lala's father standing in benign contemplation by their table. 'She insists we have been most remiss in not having you for dinner,' he continued heartily as Melik's eyes froze him to the spot, 'and won't rest now until you come over and have a glass of wine with us.'

Louisa raised her eyes past the portly figure of Lala's father to Lala herself, still sitting across the room, and just for a moment, as their eyes met, she saw concentrated poison oozing out of the sloe eyes with such malevolence that it turned her blood to water.

The rest of the evening was stone-cold misery. Somehow, when they joined Lala and her parents, the Turkish girl contrived to seat Melik at her side with Louisa placed firmly in between the aged parents who kept her busy in conversation the whole night, albeit innocently, leaving Melik to Lala's tender devices. And the devices were *very* tender. By the time Melik asked Louisa to dance when the last note of the solemn-faced guitarist had died away and the small stage had been cleared, she could have hit him. Couldn't he *see* what Lala was doing? Was he blind to the fact that she was positively devouring him with her eyes, her constant touching, or did he like it? The thought was painful. Two women interested in him and clearly at odds — did that give his male ego some sort of super-boost? He'd been playing with her. All along he'd been playing with her.

She was stiff and icy-faced in his arms, excusing herself immediately the music ended and making her way to the small cloakroom in the lobby on legs that were controlled by sheer will-power. It was with a feeling of inevitable doom that she saw Lala's small cat-like face in the mirror behind her a few seconds later.

'You are enjoying your stay in Melik's beautiful home?' Lala sat down on the tiny upholstered stool next to hers and fiddled with her immaculate hair with long, red-tipped talons.

Louisa took a long deep breath. What now? This clearly wasn't going to be a sociable little chat. 'Yes, thank you.' She continued renewing her lipstick as she had been doing when Lala entered.

'Yes, he is a good. . .host.' Lala slanted her gaze at Louisa's stiff profile. 'But then he is good at many things, is he not?' She stroked a hand down her arm dreamily. 'So many things. . .'

'If you have got something to say, Lala, say it.' Louisa swung round on her seat, her eyes blazing and her face white.

'Me?' Lala opened her eyes as wide as they would go. 'But I am making the conversation, Louisa, as my finishing school taught me. We were instructed to be gracious to those less socially acceptable than ourselves.'

'Were you?' Louisa's lip curled back in distaste as she looked down into the spoilt, cruel, beautiful face below her, and she stood up abruptly. 'It was most fortunate you were not instructed to keep silent in the presence of those who were better people than yourself or you would have lost the use of your tongue within months, wouldn't you?' Her eyes were withering as they swept over the other girl's face. 'You are without doubt, Lala, one of the most unpleasant, pathetic females I know, and undoubtedly rotten to the core.'

'You dare to talk to me like this?' Lala had sprung up as though there were springs on her feet, her high cheekbones scarlet with outrage.

'But of course,' Louisa said icily, her eyes dark with contempt. 'I was making the conversation, Lala, as *my* finishing school taught me, the finishing school of life. It taught me that people like you are ten-a-penny and just as cheap. You are worthless, quite, quite worthless.'

She was just opening the door into the lobby when the other girl's voice made her freeze for a split-second as it hissed into the stark silence left by her words. 'And you think you are so clever, that you are the one? When you lie in his arms at night and breathe in his body you think that it will last? That you can satisfy a man like him with your milk-white skin and your pale, cold heart? Well, he is mine, do you hear that? What we have shared, what we *will* share when he is tired of you and you have been sent away to your cold land across the seas, is beyond anything you could know. I tell you——'

Louisa walked through the door and let it swing shut

on the viciously vindictive tirade but as she walked
back to Melik and the others she felt physically ill. He
had slept with her, *obviously* he had slept with her, and
Lala, at least, was convinced it was not over. She hated
him. Oh, she did.

'Louisa?' Melik rose immediately she reached the
table, his eyes concerned. 'What is it? You are not
well?'

'No, I'm not, I'm sorry. . .' She turned to Lala's
parents with a wan smile. 'I seem to have developed
the most dreadful headache. . .'

'It's the lights.' Lala's father touched her arm sym-
pathetically. 'All this flashing and goodness knows
what.'

'We will go.' Melik made their goodbyes swiftly and
within minutes they were outside in the fresh, crisp air,
mercifully without seeing Lala again. 'You need medi-
cation?' He looked at her anxiously. 'Shall I get —— ?'

'I just want to be left alone.' Her control suddenly
snapped and she glared at him furiously, the hot tears
pricking at the back of her eyes in stark contrast to her
angry face. 'Especially by you! You never leave me
alone.'

'I apologise.' He had turned white at the attack, his
hand dropping like a stone from her arm.

The journey home was a nightmare she thought
would never end. Lala's poison had got into her veins
and her very bones throbbed with the words she was
desperately trying to shut out of her consciousness,
added to which the look on Melik's face, as they had
got into the car outside the hotel, had cut her to the
quick, leaving a big raw wound that was slowly seeping
blood.

But it couldn't be real, could it? There was Lala and

goodness knew how many others; that expression of stunned hurt and pain — it wasn't real, was it? *Was it?* Oh, how would she know? She didn't know anything any more and she loved him too much, hated him too much, to try and make sense of it all.

Once back in her room she lay in numb misery all night, drifting off to sleep as dawn touched the night sky and the first birds began to call tentatively into the still, clear air. By the time she had showered and ventured downstairs later in the morning Melik was already working in his study with the door firmly shut and a pile of papers had been placed on the desk in her room with written instructions in his clear, flowing hand as to how he expected her to deal with them. And so the pattern for the next few days was set. Work all day, dinner at night with the atmosphere so thick it was suffocating, and then a long, endless night of tossing and turning in between cat-naps.

She bitterly regretted her words to him outside the restaurant now but there was no way she could undo the damage they had caused. Too late she realised she had played right into Lala's manipulative little hands. He was furious with her for what he considered unreasonable and unexplainable behaviour and he had had enough. That much was clear. No doubt Lala would be quick to provide comfort. The thought made her grind her teeth in impotent rage at her mishandling of the whole miserable episode. Why did I let Lala get to me? she asked herself flatly on the morning of the seventh day as she sat gazing out of her bedroom window before going downstairs for breakfast. Why didn't I talk to him or something, anything. . .?

Because she had been frightened of what she might hear. She shut her eyes against the knowledge of her own weakness. If he had confirmed that Lala was more than a friend it might have opened a Pandora's box that she just couldn't face. But perhaps it would have been preferable to this? It was killing her to see him each day, hear his voice, and have him treat her with such careful, cold politeness. She clenched her hands into fists against the pain in her heart that was twisting her nerves into shreds.

Well, it's too late now anyway, she thought grimly as she rose and made her way to the door. He had made it clear that he was finished with her, she was just another employee now, and as soon as his business here was completed it would be back to Istanbul and he would probably request a replacement assistant. The bolt of anguish was ravaging.

As she made her way downstairs their conversation at the restaurant before Lala's father interrupted them was there in piercing clarity as it had been since it had been spoken. What had he been going to say? Had she imagined it all? She wouldn't be surprised. Her mouth twisted bitterly. She had felt more than once in the last few days that she was going crazy.

'Thank you, Safiye.' Louisa smiled warmly at the small housekeeper as she came bustling in with a covered dish that she placed in front of Louisa with a little nod. The little Turkish woman had decided that Louisa wasn't eating enough and had made it her mission in life to remedy the situation. Louisa appreciated the concern but, feeling as she did at the moment, the constant churning in her stomach made eating a necessity rather than a pleasure. However, the *menemen*, a delicious concoction of eggs, peppers, tomatoes and cheese served with small buttery buns called *pogacu* and various kinds of cheese *borek* — layered pastry leaves cooked in the oven—was very tempting and the last thing she wanted to do was to offend the housekeeper, who had shown her nothing but kindness.

'She is worried about you.' As Safiye left the room Melik glanced up from his own breakfast. 'As I am. You are not eating enough and you are too pale.'

'I'm. . .I'm fine.' It was the first personal remark he had made in days and, accompanied by the concern which had darkened the handsome, austere face and narrowed the golden eyes, it was almost too much for her over-sensitised emotions. 'Really.'

'No, you are not.' His eyes moved over her face slowly. 'Perhaps I should not have brought you here but I thought——' He stopped abruptly. 'We will be returning to Istanbul the day after tomorrow.'

The sickening jolt in her stomach allowed her to nod only. She wouldn't have trusted her voice. This was it, then, just like that.

'I want to make a detour, however, so we will actually leave here tomorrow morning, stay overnight in reserved accommodation and fly to Istanbul the following day. This is acceptable to you?' She nodded dully. 'You are not going to ask me the nature of the business? Enquire about the. . .suitability of the accommodation?' There was a note in his voice she couldn't quite place but she merely shook her head flatly, pushing the rest of the food around on her plate with her fork. She couldn't eat another bite. 'I see.' From the sharpening of the beautiful eyes it was clear he didn't but he said no more, pushing his own plate aside with a muttered oath and stalking to his study without another glance at her bent head.

It was much later, after dinner, when she was alone in her room and preparing for bed after packing her belongings and leaving the case by the door for collection by Osman first thing in the morning, that she heard the sharp tones of the doorbell. Some intuitive shiver, a little shudder down her spine, made her walk carefully to the door and open it a fraction, peering out into the darkened landing as she listened intently.

'Melik, darling. . .' Lala's voice was clear and warm and seductively throaty. 'Father told me you are leaving tomorrow; you were going to disappear back into the big bad world without telling me?'

'What are you doing here, Lala?' Louisa heard the sound of footsteps on the beautifully laid wooden floor and surmised that Melik was leading Lala into his study where a small fire had been lit earlier that evening to offset the winter chill. 'It's late.'

'I just had to see you and you know me, darling, when I want something or someone. . .' The low, suggestive, sexy laughter had been carefully cultivated for maximum effect and as it coiled up the stairs Louisa shut her door firmly, her breath a burning tight ball in her throat.

She had been so gullible! As she leant back against the carved oak door she shut her eyes tight for a moment, her heart thudding. So credulous, so stupid. . . *But it was her fault.* She opened her eyes to stare unseeing into the dimly lit room. She had begun to believe what she wanted to believe, *he* had made no promises, told no lies, assured her of nothing; in fact he had been painfully honest about his past life. She collapsed on the wide, soft bed, her head whirling. He had never uttered a word of love, anything to make her think she was any different from any other female he desired. If she had chosen to read more into the odd veiled comment, the occasional fleeting glance, well. . .that was her mistake. He had talked of possession, of branding her as his, of fierce desire, but never, ever love. . .

It was very late when she heard Lala's jeep roar off into the night and she felt very cold. Cold and curiously numb.

CHAPTER TEN

'You still haven't asked.'

'I'm sorry?' She came out of the blackness of her thoughts to find Melik's eyes tight on her face.

He indicated the lush green mountainous terrain beneath the small aircraft with a wave of his hand. 'Where we are going. You are not in the least bit curious?'

'Should I be?' she asked flatly. 'I suppose it's estate business——'

'No, it is not estate business,' he said softly. 'It is Melik and Louisa business.'

'Now look here——' She had thought nothing could permeate the aura of misery that had settled on her the night before like a big dark cloud but he had accomplished it with just a few quiet words and a warm smile. How *dared* he smile like that at her, when he and Lala had been huddled together half the night. . .? How *dared* he?

'No, I will look nowhere.' His face had changed at the glare on hers but his voice was still quiet, beautifully controlled. 'I am taking you to see a ceremony, a very special ceremony that only happens once a year, that is all. I am not abducting you for dire purposes or locking you away in a dark fortress somewhere, although I would be lying if I didn't admit the thought had occurred to me more than once lately. However——' he took a long deep breath ' —there is an old Turkish proverb that I have found most com-

161

forting in the last few weeks. A rough translation would
be that the prize is all the more precious when it has
been gained on the blood of the winner. Do you follow
me?'

'I haven't the faintest idea what you are talking
about,' she said in all honesty, her face still scarlet with
anger.

'No?' His eyes wandered over her hot face linger-
ingly. 'Such an unkind little tigress not even to notice
when the sharp claws draw blood, but it will make the
taming of you all the sweeter, my pet.'

'I am not your pet!' The low, fierce retort was filled
with such enmity that his brow wrinkled against it.
'And you are beyond belief, Melik Haman; I ——'

'Look down there.' He had completely ignored her
words with such regal disdain that she didn't know
whether to hit him or scream. 'We are flying over the
Göreme region now; I will take you there one day. It
is the strange country of the Christian troglodytes; do
you remember me mentioning them?'

She nodded her head tightly, her eyes blazing.

'This whole region is a uniquely spectacular volcanic
maze of giant cones and chimneys of yellow tufa that
are above the general level of land,' he continued
urbanely, quite unmoved by her rage, 'and in some of
the fields of red and yellow volcanic earth the peasant
land-owners have small plots of vines and fruit trees
with some of the bigger cones being cut to form
waterproof storerooms for their crops.'

'Look, Melik ——'

'The ones directly below are several storeys high,' he
said evenly, 'and still inhabited today. I understand
modern porches and steps have been added in the most
sohisticated ones. And in Kaymakli and Derinkuyu,

which we shall be reaching shortly, there are vast underground cities where at the dawn of Christianity the early Christians sheltered from persecution.'

'I'm not interested in underground cities,' she said sharply, her voice shaking with rage. 'What I want to know is——'

'You aren't interested?' His voice was mockingly shocked. 'And I thought I was the savage? You mean to say the fact that there are churches, palaces, whole villages intricately planned and descending to a hundred and twenty metres below the ground surface does not even flood your mind with just a little wonder? How sad. . .' He eyed her wickedly. 'I am in the company of a philistine. The human moles that inhabited the underground catacombs would not thank you for such cool uninterest, my superior little English rose.'

'I'm warning you, Melik——' She stopped abruptly as he placed a finger on her lips, his eyes dancing.

'I like to make you mad, Louisa; you were born for such sport.' He settled back in his seat comfortably without taking his eyes off her face. 'This cold icicle that has been wandering round my house for the last few days, that is not you.'

'You know nothing about me, Melik, nothing at all,' she said hotly as the sense of outrage and unfairness swamped all other emotion.

'This is perhaps a little true.' He eyed her consideringly. 'But I know all I need to know is here——' he touched his chest lightly '—in my heart. The rest?' He shrugged slowly. 'The rest can be told if you wish it; if not. . .'

'That is very magnanimous of you,' she said scathingly as the image of Lala flashed on to the screen of her mind. 'Do you mean to say you accept all your women at face value? Isn't that a little dangerous?'

'I have survived, as you see,' he said with irritating composure. 'But as to all these other women. . .' The golden eyes narrowed. 'I am neither a fool nor a careless man, Louisa, as I thought you knew. I was born into great wealth and with such blessing comes a heightened sense of one's own worth. I have known exactly what most of the women I have been involved with wanted and let us say the appeal of my body was somewhat outshone by the size of my bank balance.'

'But if you knew that. . .' She faltered to a halt. 'I mean, why get involved with them, then?'

He shrugged lightly. 'I am a man, not a monk. If that answer displeases you I can tell you in all honesty it is the first time I have wished it could be different. But I cannot lie to you. My only plea for mitigation would be. . .' He hesitated.

'Yes?'

'I realise now I was searching for something that I wanted without being sure if it even existed. Does that make sense?'

'No.' She stared at him in confusion.

'And then I found it,' he said softly. 'The pearl beyond price. But the shell is still tightly hiding the full beauty from coming forth, but shells were made to be broken. . .'

'We shall be landing in just under ten minutes, sir.' Osman's expressionless voice sounded over their heads. 'There will be a car to meet you and I will be here at the same time tomorrow.'

The interruption seemed to signal the end of further conversation and as Melik settled back in his seat his face was enigmatic and still, his big body relaxed as the plane flew on in the clear blue sky. When they left its warm protection a short time later the first thing Louisa noticed was the remarkable change in temperature. After leaving the wet, temperate region of the Black Sea the sharp cold of the Anatolian plateau was striking.

It was as though they were in a different country, Louisa thought as the hired car sped them onwards, surveying the plain of Konya that fanned out from the foothills of the Taurus Mountains into vast bleakness. 'In ancient Neolithic times the wild bull and leopard wandered these grasslands,' Melik said softly in her ear, 'and Konya itself is a very old city, an oasis of commerce in this massive wilderness.'

'And the celebration?' She was vitally conscious of his hard thigh next to hers in the close confines of the car, the big bulk of him next to her causing a trembling in her stomach that she had learnt weeks ago was impossible to control.

'Ah, the whirling dervishes,' he said thoughtfully. 'It is a ceremony to commemorate the death of Mevlana, who founded the order. You would have approved of him, I think.'

'Would I?' She looked at him in surprise. 'Why?'

'His basic philosophy consisted of equality for the sexes —' he shot her a wry glance '—the pursuit of righteousness and communion with God, which especially in those times, the 1200s, was quite radical. He was married to one woman all his life and preached passionately that such faithfulness was right, that all women as well as men should be free.'

'Did he?' She was warming to Mevlana already.

The city itself was very Islamic and very beautiful, and their hotel was situated in the area of the main square, Hukumet Meydani, both gracious and comfortable. 'Your key.' As Melik handed her the small metal object she caught the cynical gleam in his eyes. 'Did you expect a key of your very own?'

She knew what he was asking and kept her face bland. 'Of course. How else would I lock my door?'

He laughed softly, his eyes glittering. 'Of course, how else?' Dressed as he was in casual trousers and a thick black leather jacket, he looked overwhelmingly attractive, and as her heart thudded a little quicker he stroked her hot cheek with a thoughtful finger. 'How long, my tigress? How long before there is only one key?' It wasn't really a question and she made no attempt to answer it.

It was with some trepidation that she got ready later that afternoon for dinner with Melik before the ceremony began. They had spent the day sightseeing and she had found the ancient city, a prosperous route and market centre for the last two thousand years, absorbing. The Alaeddin Mosque, one of the oldest in Turkey, with its wooden roofing supported by forty-two Roman columns and intricately carved pulpit and altar, was beautiful as would befit a building holding the mortal remains of eight sultans, and the other Seljuk monuments to architecture equally so, but it was the Mevlana Mausoleum, the old monastery where the order of dervishes was founded, that really gripped her interest.

Dominated by a conical, turquoise-blue dome, it was a landmark in the city, and the museum hall where the ritual dances used to take place contained priceless seven-hundred-year-old carpets, manuscripts, musical instruments, dervish garments and prayer rugs, and even, allegedly, part of Mahomet's beard. As she stood there, Melik's arm resting lightly round her waist and the aura of the East stronger than she had ever known it, Louisa was vitally aware, with a painful clarity that gripped at her throat, that soon all this would just be a memory and she would be gone. Gone from this land of arid plains and lush forests, dramatic mountains and peaceful lakes, this land of exquisitely beautiful ancient mosques and sultans' palaces, tiny fishing villages and small country towns where life had remained the same for thousands of years; and gone from this man. This ruthless, cold man who could be as gentle as a kitten and as fierce as a wild animal almost in the same breath.

'Louisa?' The knock at her door brought her eyes snapping to the mirror as she checked her hair and light make-up. The smart but casual pale blue wool dress would carry her with equal sureness into a poor café or sophisticated restaurant, and the matching coat was not only functional but extremely warm, which, as the ceremony was held in front of the old monastery, she felt was more than necessary.

'You look gorgeous.' As she opened the door he moved her back into the room, taking her in his arms before she could guess his intention and straining her to him in an agony of a kiss that not only bruised her lips but tore at her heart. Had he kissed Lala like this last night before she had left? Had Lala drunk in the feel and smell of him, the intoxicating thrill of being held next to the heart of a man who was all male and unashamedly dangerous? 'Louisa. . .' As she felt her head begin to swim she was horrified to find she wanted to kiss him back, wanted the penetrating invasion of his mouth, the hard jut of his body, the overwhelming warmth of his lovemaking. . .

'Don't!' She jerked backwards and he made no attempt to stop her, turning and walking past her to hold back the flimsy curtains and stare down into the street below for long minutes, his back rigid and straight and his head stiff as though he was fighting for control.

'I'm sorry.' As he turned she saw he was his old cynical self again, his eyes hooded and his mouth sardonic. 'But that perfume you have on is the very devil.'

She met the veiled eyes and managed a small smile. 'It should be. It costs me a week's wages. It's called Enticement.'

'It works.'

He walked across the room and picked up a small package he had slipped on the table by the door as he had entered. 'Here.'

'What is it?'

'Not again.' He closed his eyes briefly. 'I really must give you lessons on how to accept gifts gracefully, when I have the time, along with a few other instructions on a topic dearer to my heart.' He eyed her wickedly and she found she had unwrapped the tiny parcel without knowing it.

'Oh, how pretty.' The perfect magnolia bloom was encased in a small transparent box that opened from the top, and as Melik lifted the corsage from its tissue the heady perfume emanating from the pure white petals filled the room.

'Let me.' He fixed the exquisite flower to her dress, just above her breast, and although the touch of his hand was making her limp she forced herself to stand perfectly still until he had finished. 'The white flower signifies innocence, virginity,' he continued softly as he gazed down into the brown darkness of her eyes, 'and this is how I see you, Louisa. I do not care about what has happened in your past,' he went on quietly as she went to speak, 'or how this thing that has hurt you may have involved another man. No, that is not quite true.' A small muscle clenched in his jaw for a moment. 'I care — hell, I care; it's ripped me apart night after night thinking that he may have hurt you, abused you — '

'Melik — ' She was horrified by the savage pain in his eyes but as she spoke he took a deep, shuddering breath, forcing back the control with iron determination.

'But I want you to know that he can't touch you if you don't let him, not here, inside, where it counts.' He touched her heart gently. 'This flower is how I see you, Louisa, pure, beautiful and without blemish.'

'Melik, please. . .' She shut her eyes as the tears she had been holding back for minutes squeezed underneath her lids. 'Please don't.'

'No tears.' He touched her face softly. 'And no confessions. Be it a man or something else, I care only as much as it has hurt you. And now we go.'

The rest of the evening was bittersweet. They dined at the hotel and as they left the air was frosty and bitterly cold to their warm faces. As Melik pulled her closely into the crook of her arm Louisa knew, with a surety that stopped her heart, that this would have to be the end. Once in Istanbul she would fly back to England immediately, because if she stayed any longer within his orbit she would become anything he wanted her to become, do anything he wanted her to do, forget her scruples, her innate desperation for a relationship that excluded a third or fourth or fifth party, and he was from a different culture, a different world — he

probably didn't even comprehend why she would want
to be the only one; Lala showed that.

The ceremony was eerie and beautiful and strange
and the religious dance, accompanied by musicians
wearing tall red tarbushes, was intricately fascinating.
Accompanied by the ethereal sound of reed flutes, the
whirling men in their long white robes and long hats
symbolising their own gravestones told their story of
the shedding of all earthly ties in their quest for union
with God.

'Each dancer is holding his right palm towards
heaven to receive a blessing and his left palm down to
distribute it upon the earth,' Melik whispered in her
ear as they stood in the crowd in awestruck silence.

'How do you know? Have you been before?' she
whispered back and he nodded slowly, his eyes fixed
on the figures as they spun on bare heels with sublime
speed and ease, the spotlights turning their robes
different monochrome colours as the skirts billowed
outwards. Whom had he brought that time? She hated
the dart of jealousy that bit at her mind with viciously
sharp teeth. Had it been Lala?

'I brought my mother a few years ago,' he said
quietly. 'Amazingly, in spite of living most of her life
in this country, she had never come before.' He flashed
her a quick smile. 'Crazy, eh?'

So she had been wrong. Her thoughts ran on and
then shuddered to a halt. But a future with this man,
however short it might be, would hold the same
piercing thoughts. Not about the past, she could accept
and forget that, but every time he left, every time he
waved goodbye, she would wonder who he was going
to.

'The big circle they are standing in demonstrates

wheels within wheels,' Melik continued softly, quite oblivious to her inward turmoil. 'The movements of the stars in the cosmos and the soul's search for truth.' The dancers were making her feel dizzy; she couldn't believe that they could remain upright, let alone whirl at such breathtaking speed and with such superhuman control. On and on they went, the shroud-like skirts forming a cone and the men's faces transfixed as though they had fallen into a trance.

As the scent from the blossom fixed to her dress mingled with the enormity of the obvious dedication of the dancers Louisa began to feel that the whole evening wasn't quite real, but even as the poignant ceremony drew to an end and a man began chanting passages from the Koran she knew she had come to a decision. She would tell him tonight she had to leave, return to England. She owed him that honesty at least after the gentleness he had portrayed with the flower and his care for her feelings, however much pain he had given her.

'Melik?' As they wandered back to the hotel, part of a vast crowd, she knew the moment had come. She couldn't tell him when they were alone, she just couldn't.

'Yes?'

'I'm going back to England when we return to Istanbul.'

'You are joking.' The tone was flat but she went on.

'I need to get away.' He had stiffened at her side but she couldn't stop now.

'From me?'

'Partly.' She tried to make her voice firm.

'May I ask why?' His voice was cold now, cold and formal.

'Because I can't be what you want me to be; I'm not made like you, it's as simple as that.' She glanced at his face and then looked away quickly, shaken by the darkness moulding the strong features into a devil's mask.

'Meaning?'

He wasn't going to make this easy, she thought painfully. 'I know you want a relationship with me,' she said slowly, 'but that sort of thing, it wouldn't be enough for me. I'd want more and I know you wouldn't.'

'You know?' His voice was deceptively soft. 'What do you think I would want of you exactly, Louisa?'

'We both know that; I don't need to spell it out,' she said tightly. 'You can have affairs without it meaning too much to you; you *told* me that, like with Lala.'

'Lala?' He stopped dead and turned her to him, his eyes golden shafts of light in the dark brown of his face. 'What has Lala got to do with anything?'

'Well, she's ——' She stopped abruptly, taken aback by the fury in his face. 'I mean ——'

'You think Lala is my mistress?' he hissed slowly. 'You think I would insult you by asking you to my home and then parading another woman in front of you, not to mention the betrayal of friendship such a relationship would entail with her parents? That is the sort of man you think I am?'

'But she said ——' She stopped abruptly. What had Lala said, now? She had never actually stated bald facts; it had been all suggestion and innuendo.

'Lala is a spoilt child who plays at being grown-up,' Melik said with icy coldness. 'She is the troublesome little sister I never had. That is all.'

'It might be all to you but it certainly isn't like that

with her,' Louisa said quickly as the piercingly sharp
flood of relief that had flooded her body for a few
seconds at his words died at the blackness of his face.
'She said——'

'I do not care what she said,' Melik said furiously,
giving her a little shake that earned a few interested
glances from passers-by. 'You could have asked me
about it, couldn't you? Talked to me? Treated me as a
human being for once? But no, I am not such a thing
in your eyes, am I? Exactly how do you see me,
Louisa, as an animal, an object or worse?'

'Melik——'

'I have had enough.' He took a step backwards from
her as though she were suddenly unclean. 'It is not just
Lala, is it? You think I am some sort of over-sexed
savage who has women in every place. Yes?' Her face
was scarlet now; she had never seen him like this
before and it frightened her. 'Never has anyone dared
to say such things before. You think I am incapable of
normal commitment in spite of all I have tried to tell
you, the way I feel——' He stopped abruptly as a spasm
of pain cut through the steel in his eyes. 'You *should*
go home to England, Louisa.' he drew himself up very
straight, his big body iron-hard. 'This is exactly what
you should do.'

How they reached the hotel she never did know; the
journey forever remained a blank in her mind. Her
whole being was consumed with the sickening dread
that she had just made the biggest mistake of her life.
He saw her to her room with icy politeness, careful not
to touch her or even brush against her. 'Goodnight.'
He inclined his dark head with arctic courtesy and
as he began to walk away she thought her heart
would break.

'Melik?'

He paused for a moment, his back rigid, and then walked on, his broad shoulders set and his head high.

That was it. As she closed the door and sank down on the bed her mind searched frantically for a way to undo the damage. . .but there was none. She closed her eyes helplessly. And he didn't even know she loved him.

The journey to Istanbul was tense and painful and by the time Louisa reached her flat, Melik seeing her to the door and depositing her case just inside, declining the offer of coffee with a stiff, 'No, thank you,' she felt like a wet rag. She hadn't closed her eyes the night before, sitting by the low arched windowsill that had looked out on to the road underneath and waiting for the first glow of dawn to break the black sky. When the first wailing call from the mosque minaret loud-speakers had summoned the faithful to prayer she had risen slowly, showering and washing her hair with leaden, sluggish movements as though she were weak and frail after recovering from a major operation, before getting dressed and resuming her seat by the window as the big city had come to life.

'I would suggest you have a light lunch and rest this afternoon,' he had said distantly as Osman drove them to her flat. 'The office will wait.'

'I'll see.' She had been staring out of the window into the muggy December day and hadn't turned her eyes to his, missing the swift piercing glance of concern he had given her white face. 'I might come in just to sort my desk; it's bound to be piled high.'

'Call the office and I'll send Osman if you decide to do that.'

She had nodded slowly, her eyes lifeless, while the mad whirl of Istanbul traffic had screeched noisily beyond the car's quiet interior, making Melik's peaceful, gracious home seem a million miles away.

After fixing herself a quick omelette she pushed it around on the plate for a few minutes before tipping the congealed mass into the bin, forcing herself to drink two strong cups of coffee as she brushed her hair into shining order, securing it firmly in the clips Melik hated so much. She needed to look her most efficient when she approached Mrs Jones about a return ticket this afternoon. It wouldn't be a pleasant interview. She shook her head in slight surprise as she suddenly realised that the thought didn't have the power to bother her an iota. She didn't care about Mrs Jones, about Lectron, about her job; all she cared about was—— She stopped her mind from continuing. She had made her decision, burnt her boats; *there was no looking back*.

The statement mocked her as she drove to the office by dolmuş in the early afternoon drizzle that had settled on the city. No looking back? She was going to spend the rest of her life regretting she had ever set foot in this beautiful wild land.

'Miss Collins.' Mrs Jones's smile was of the hundred-watt variety and Louisa blinked a little at the older woman's enthusiasm. 'Mr Haman said we wouldn't be seeing you until tomorrow.' There was something in the older woman's attitude that Louisa couldn't quite pin down, but she was too friendly, too effusive. . .

'I wanted to talk to you, Mrs Jones,' Louisa said quietly, 'and I also thought I should put my desk in order.'

'Talk to me?' Again there was that fleeting sense of

disquiet but Louisa brushed it aside; she was imagining the apprehension in Mrs Jones's hard grey eyes. 'Well, this might be a good moment, Miss Collins; everyone has gone to lunch.'

Louisa nodded slowly. She might as well get it over with.

As she followed Mrs Jones into Mr Ashton's outer office where the secretary had her desk she mentally prepared her opening sentence. I'm afraid that due to unforeseen circumstances I shall have to return to England before Christmas, Mrs Jones. . .

'Now.' Mrs Jones indicated a seat in front of her desk as she sat down. 'I gather you've picked up on the credit problem? Well, it was only a matter of time.'

'I'm sorry?' Louisa stared at her in surprise.

'Lectron's little money-flow difficulty.' Mrs Jones smiled conspiratorially. 'I was meaning to have a word with you before Mr Haman whisked you away so suddenly. It's all in hand, my dear; there is nothing to be concerned about.'

'I'm sorry, Mrs Jones, but I don't have the faintest idea what you mean,' Louisa said helplessly. 'Is there some sort of financial problem?'

'You mean you haven't. . .?' Mrs Jones surveyed her carefully. 'Well, you soon would have.'

'Would have what?' It was becoming more like *Alice in Wonderland* every moment, Louisa thought dazedly.

'Would have realised that Lectron is short of a considerable amount of money,' Mrs Jones said quietly. 'But, as I say, it's all in hand. This little. . . complication was foreseen before we arrived here and measures have been taken.'

'Measures?' Louisa stared at the older woman's face blankly. 'What measures?'

'You must understand, Miss Collins.' Mrs Jones gave her the million-dollar smile again. 'It's all to Mr Haman's advantage in the long run. He might be covering. . .more than he envisaged now but the future of this project is worth it. He will make a great deal of money long term.'

'Yes. . .' There was still something here she didn't understand, Louisa thought uncertainly, something not quite right. 'Well, if he's happy with that I suppose all's well.'

'Ah. . .now I didn't say that, did I?' The smile dimmed a little. 'In fact I would prefer you not to bring the matter to Mr Haman's attention. There is no need.'

'He doesn't know?' Now things were beginning to make sense. 'You mean Lectron is trying to pull a fast one?'

'"Pull a fast one"?' Mrs Jones's thin mouth showed her distaste for the crudity of the expression. 'Not at all, Miss Collins; we are just. . .manipulating the facts a little.'

'Cheating him.' Louisa's voice was flat.

'Don't be so ridiculous, girl!' As the steel-grey eyes narrowed Mrs Jones reverted to type. 'Do you think Lectron could miss the chance to establish themselves out here in Turkey just because of the short-sightedness of certain banks?'

'You are talking about fraud, Mrs Jones.'

'How dare you?' Mrs Jones stood up and moved round her desk to stand in front of Louisa, the angular face fairly quivering with indignation. 'Why do you think you were chosen to replace Beryl, you stupid girl? We thought we could rely on your discretion; you have always been a model employee —— '

'As I shall continue to be for however long I work

for Lectron, Mrs Jones.' Louisa glared up at the red face angrily. 'But that does not include lying and deceiving Mr Haman. Just the opposite, in fact.'

'I'm just asking you to keep quiet.' Mrs Jones's voice was threatening now and very cold. 'If you don't Mr Haman would never believe you didn't know exactly what was going on from the very beginning and you will find yourself minus a job here and also in England. References can be. . .delicate things, Miss Collins.'

'Get lost, Mrs Jones.' It was said with such quietness that for a second the import of the softly spoken words didn't register on the older woman's face. 'If you think for one minute I'm letting Melik carry more than his fair share you're wrong.' She too had risen to glare straight into Mrs Jones's tight face. 'He is worth a hundred of any of you; there isn't a deceitful bone in his body, and if you think you can pull the wool over his eyes and ask me to keep quiet then you're wrong. I won't do it.'

'You'll regret it; I'll see to it that your job——'

'And you know exactly what you can do with your precious job, don't you?' As she pushed past Mrs Jones's square body she stopped dead to see Melik in front of her, the dark face stunned and incredulous as his eyes flashed from her to Mrs Jones, who sank down into the chair Louisa had vacated with a little whimper when she caught sight of the big figure in the doorway.

'I'll deal with you later.' The deep voice was deadly and Mrs Jones sank further into the upholstery, her face ashen.

'Melik——' As Louisa went to speak she found herself whisked at great speed out of the main office, which was beginning to fill with staff, and down the stairs outside, her feet barely able to touch the floor.

'Melik ——'

'Quiet; not now.'

She tried to glance up at him, to see his face, but they were flying along the pavement outside so fast that it was all she could do to get her breath, and then suddenly, thankfully, they were in one of the tiny squares dotted about Istanbul where a few pigeons were being fed by two old men and a group of children and the wailing rhythm of a Turkish pop song drifted lazily from an open window in one of the houses surrounding the square. 'Sit down.'

As he pushed her on to a small wooden bench and sat down beside her she glanced at his expressionless face anxiously. Did he think she had been in on the scheme to cheat him? How much had he heard? Did he even know what they had been talking about? And oh—her stomach knotted tightly—he did look *good*.

'It's truth time.' He turned to face her and she saw that his eyes were brilliantly iridescent, the flecks of green standing out in striking contrast to the dark, tawny surround. 'Why did you say all that to Mrs Jones?'

'Because I didn't know what was going on,' she said faintly. 'I ——'

'I don't mean that!' He flicked his hand savagely. 'I know you wouldn't be involved in anything underhand; that is not in question. I mean about me, being worth a hundred of them. . .' There was something in his face that tore at her heart and melted all her pride, her carefully built-up self-protection, leaving her wide open, vulnerable. He had said it was truth time. Well, so be it.

'Because you are,' she said simply.

'Louisa ——' He stopped abruptly, his hand reaching

out to touch her and then freezing in mid-air to fall
back to his side. 'Hell, I don't know what to say to
you.' There was a deep pleading in the proud face, a
brokenness, that she had never imagined seeing there.
'I don't know what you want.'

'I want you.' As she said it, finally, *finally* said it,
everything fell into place. She loved him. She couldn't
exist without him. If it meant sharing him. . .well, she
would face that when it happened and go from there;
at the very least she would have precious memories to
cling on to.

'You don't know what you're saying.' It wasn't the
response she expected and she stared at him in surprise.
'Dammit, woman, you don't even *like* me.'

'I love you, Melik.' If he wanted it all, the last ounce
of pride, it was his. 'I always have.'

'Louisa.' He pulled her to him with such violence
that the pigeons scattered in a great whirling cloud and
the old men hurried the children off into a secluded
corner of the square where they tut-tutted at the fallen
standards of the young. He didn't kiss her, merely
holding her close to the pounding fury of his heart with
such savage intensity that she really did feel he was
crushing her bones.

'Melik——' At the first wriggle she was free. 'I want
to explain——'

'No!' His voice was violent. 'I don't want to hear. I
just want to sit here and for you to tell me that you
love me again and again and again until I can take it
in. If you knew what you've put me through——'

'I have to tell you.' She placed a small hand on his
chest and the shudder that racked his body trembled
through hers.

'It's not necessary.' He touched her face and then

pulled her to him again, kissing her desperately, frantically, as though he would never have his fill of her lips, his body rigid with the control he was exercising. 'If we were anywhere but here. . .' He eyed her hotly. 'I want you, now.'

'Listen.' She moved a body's breadth away and began to talk, baring her heart, her soul, and he listened, quietly and without interrupting, although as she mentioned Oliver his face stiffened for a second before relaxing again, a compassion washing over the austere features that caught at her breath. She told him about the childhood years, the loneliness, the desperate feeling of being unloved, unlovable, and the damage it had caused to a sensitive, highly responsive nature that had gradually closed in on itself for protection. And her face told him much more than she realised as she felt her way through the years until she stopped, bruised and shaken by some of the deeply buried memories she had brought to the surface.

'I could kill them.' His voice was low and painful. 'They are your parents but I could kill them. Have they any idea, now, what they did to you? What they are still doing?'

'Not still doing.' As she touched her hand to his face he caught it and pressed her fingers tightly to his mouth. 'Not now I've met you.'

'And Oliver?' The beautiful eyes stroked probingly over her face. 'You have peace now about Oliver?'

'Yes.' She met his gaze squarely. 'I felt guilty that what I felt for him was so lukewarm beside you but I know now that that was another time, another place, and he was happy with things the way they were. He wasn't a. . .physical man,' she said haltingly.

'Not a physical man?' He frowned slowly. 'You

mean——?' He gazed at her, a dawning incredulity in his eyes. 'You don't mean——'

'We never made love.' It was good that she could give him this one gift, very good. 'I've never made love with anyone.'

'But——' He shook his head wonderingly, unable to speak. 'I cannot believe, looking as you do. . . When I think of how I rushed you, frightened you. . .' A darkness came into his face. 'You should have said, my love; forgive me.'

'There is nothing to forgive, Melik, and you didn't frighten me.' A small smile touched her mouth at the almost comical tragedy in his. 'I liked it.'

'You did?' The thickening of his voice sent hot colour flooding into her cheeks. 'Oh, Louisa. . .I love you, more than life, more than I had ever imagined it was possible to love. You will marry me, *soon*?'

'Marry you?' She stared at him in amazement. 'You want to *marry* me?'

'Of course.' He raised his head proudly. 'What did you think I was offering you?'

'Well, I don't know, this country. . . Your customs are different here; I wasn't sure. . .'

'Louisa, I have never wanted to marry anyone before and if you refused me I never would again. When you become my wife, if you accept me, our hearts will become one, beat as one. I shall never want another; can you believe that?'

'I want to.' She touched the hard contours of his face tenderly. 'But you must understand, Melik, I find it hard to think anyone can love me, let alone someone like you.'

'Someone like me?' The incredulity was back in his face. 'But I am not worthy to be dust under your feet, my love; how can you ever think——?' He stopped abruptly. 'But I will spend the rest of my life convincing you, Louisa. You remember that first day at the office, when I took you out for lunch and we visited the Topkapi Palace, the Harem?'

'Yes.'

'And I told you the story of the favourite, the one woman who could tame the wild heart of the Sultan until she was the only one he desired, the one he gave absolute sovereign power to, the jewel of his life?'

'Melik——'

'You are the one, Louisa. You are my heart, my blood, my life. There will never be anyone else; you are my destiny.'

'Your destiny?' She stared in wonder at the passionate warmth in his face.

'And the future is ours, my sweet tigress, all ours. . .'

Welcome to Europe

TURKEY — 'The Cradle of Civilisation'

Turkey is a unique country, straddling two continents — Europe and Asia. It's always been a crossroads for travellers and conquerors, and so it's no surprise that it has a truly magnificent past, and is full of historic treasures from succeeding civilisations. Even someone who spends just a short time in Turkey can sample something of its amazing history. . .but it's also a paradise of sun, sea and sand, ideal for the beach holiday of your dreams! Or, for that matter, you can explore the lovely countryside, or even ski on the spectacular mountains. Who could ask for more. . .?

THE ROMANTIC PAST

Turkey has seen the rise and fall of many successive empires, Persia, Rome and Byzantium among them. 'The world's first town', a Neolithic city dating back to around 6500 BC, is situated here, and in later times the Romans in particular built magnificent and wealthy cities which can still be seen in all the splendour of their decay. But one of the most romantic chapters of Turkish history concerns the ancient city of **Troy**. The legend—and the great poet **Homer's** *Iliad*—tells how **Paris**, son of Priam, King of Troy, abducted the beautiful **Helen**, wife of King Menelaus of Sparta, and took her back to his city. The Greek princes followed, and besieged Troy for ten years, finally capturing it only by a trick: they pretended to give up and leave, but hid themselves, fully armed, in a huge hollow **wooden horse**, which the unsuspecting Trojans took into the city. The warriors appeared while the Trojans were celebrating and destroyed the city and killed or enslaved its inhabitants.

The story of Troy has been told and retold throughout the world for thousands of years, but in the nineteenth century the German romantic **Heinrich Schliemann** became convinced that Homer's tale was more than just legend. He retired from business, studied archaeology, and eventually set off for Turkey to excavate at the spot which, he believed, hid the site of Troy! He did indeed find a great city which had been destroyed by fire and invasion at least once. He also found a hoard of golden treasure which he decided must be 'the jewels of Helen'—and with which he adorned his beautiful young Greek wife! The treasure has since mysteriously disappeared. . .but the ruins of Troy (or **Truva**) can still be visited—in fact, a good time to go would be during the annual festival, in August, which brings the ancient city to life.

THE ROMANTIC PRESENT — pastimes for lovers. . .

Every part of Turkey has something to delight the visitor, from the incredibly well preserved Greek and Roman city of **Pergamum**, with its library, theatre, temples and museums, to the fantastic beaches and the haunting beauty of the mountains and lakes. But most visitors will find themselves sooner or later in the city of **Istanbul**. The city, known once as **Byzantium**, was founded around 660 BC and renamed **Constantinople** when Constantine the Great made it the capital of the Roman Empire. When the Western half of the Empire was overrun by invaders, Constantinople in the East stood firm, and became, as it remains, one of the great cities of the world. Whatever name you know it by, it's certainly worth a visit!

One of the most famous sights is the **Topkapi Palace**, the maze of buildings that was the great palace of the Ottoman sultans from the fifteenth to the nineteenth centuries. It now houses a museum, with treasures which include the sultans' jewels — you may be tempted by memories of the film *Topkapi*, in which a gang of thieves attempts to steal some of them! To divert your mind from such dangerous ideas, you can also visit the fascinating **Harem**, where the hundreds of wives and concubines of the sultans lived out their lives. . .

Another world-renowned sight is the **Blue Mosque**, or Sultan Ahmet Mosque, built between 1609 and 1616. Its unrivalled silhouette has six minarets, and the stunning interior is decorated with blue tiles — hence the name. During the tourist season there is a spectacular light and sound show in the evening.

The city has many other mosques, palaces and museums for the visitor to enjoy, but there's also plenty to do out of doors; Istanbul has many picturesque squares in which you can just sit and watch the world go by. It's also a walled city — the fortifications were built in the fifth century AD by the Emperor Theodosius, and they have been fully restored to their former splendour in some places. The whole area has been declared (by UNESCO) one of the most important cultural treasures in the world.

A stay in Istanbul is not complete without a romantic excursion by boat along the *Boğazi*, or Bosporus, the narrow straits separating the two continents. The shore is a delightful mixture of old and new that typifies the city: modern hotels set next to old wooden houses, palaces or ancient ruins, pleasure gardens or intriguing markets selling art and crafts. For Istanbul must be one of the shopping capitals of the world! Most people know that it's the only place to visit for reasonably priced **leather goods**. You can choose whether to browse in atmospheric old bazaars or up-to-the-minute shops — wherever you go, you're sure to find not only leather and suede but also **jewellery**, **embroidery**, hand-painted **ceramics**, **onyx** ware and lovingly hand-crafted souvenirs of all kinds. There are also many second-hand markets where you may pick up a real bargain! If you can't resist a traditional Turkish **carpet**, remember to haggle for it — and don't forget to keep your proof of purchase, which you'll need to take it out of the country.

Turkey takes pride in keeping alive its old traditions. Its traditional sport is **'grease wrestling'**, so called because the participants smear themselves with oil so that their opponents can't get a grip on them! On a gentler note, you might be lucky enough to see a display of one of the many colourful **folk dances**, often commemorating ancient battles and other passages from history.

Turkish food is famous throughout the world. In coastal areas the **fish** and **seafood** are especially delicious, but there's also an enormous range of meat and chicken dishes. And to finish, of course, strong **Turkish coffee** and sinfully rich **pastries**! Turkey produces many excellent wines, but the real local speciality is **raki**, or 'lion's milk', which is distilled from grapes and usually mixed with water to give a cloudy appearance.

DID YOU KNOW THAT. . .?

*   **Agatha Christie** wrote the famous *Murder on the Orient Express* while staying in Istanbul.

*   Istanbul is the only city in the world built on **two continents**.

*   the Turks are particularly fond of celebrating **festivals**—there is an annual **children's festival** featuring children from all over the world. There are cultural and artistic festivals of all kinds, and, in one region, a festival of **walking sticks**—it may sound odd but they are in fact painstakingly crafted examples of traditional wood work. There's also a **camel-wrestling festival** in the winter. . .

* although Turkey is a predominantly **Muslim** country, it is a secular state which guarantees religious freedom to its inhabitants.

* the capital of Turkey is not Istanbul — it's **Ankara**.

* the Turkish currency is the **lira**.

Full of Eastern Passion...

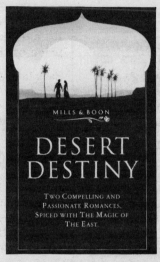

Savour the romance of the East this summer with
our two full-length compelling Romances,
wrapped together in one exciting volume.

AVAILABLE FROM 29 JULY 1994   PRICED £3.99

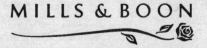

Accept 4 FREE Romances and 2 FREE gifts

FROM READER SERVICE

Here's an irresistible invitation from Mills & Boon. Please accept our offer of 4 FREE Romances, a CUDDLY TEDDY and a special MYSTERY GIFT! Then, if you choose, go on to enjoy 6 captivating Romances every month for just £1.90 each, postage and packing FREE. Plus our FREE Newsletter with author news, competitions and much more.

Send the coupon below to: Mills & Boon Reader Service, FREEPOST, PO Box 236, Croydon, Surrey CR9 9EL.

- - - - NO STAMP REQUIRED - - - - - - - - - - - - - - -

Yes! Please rush me 4 FREE Romances and 2 FREE gifts! Please also reserve me a Reader Service subscription. If I decide to subscribe I can look forward to receiving 6 brand new Romances for just £11.40 each month, post and packing FREE. If I decide not to subscribe I shall write to you within 10 days - I can keep the free books and gifts whatever I choose. I may cancel or suspend my subscription at any time. I am over 18 years of age.

Ms/Mrs/Miss/Mr _____ EP70R

Address _____

_____

Postcode _____ Signature _____

mps
MAILING
PREFERENCE
SERVICE